melville house classics

MICHAEL KOHLHAAS

MICHAEL KOHLHAAS

HEINRICH VON KLEIST

TRANSLATED BY MARTIN GREENBERG

MELVILLE HOUSE PUBLISHING
HOBOKEN, NEW JERSEY

"MICHAEL KOHLHAAS" WAS FIRST PUBLISHED IN 1810

TRANSLATION ©1960 MARTIN GREENBERG AND CRITERION BOOKS
BOOK DESIGN: DAVID KONOPKA

MELVILLE HOUSE PUBLISHING
300 OBSERVER HIGHWAY
THIRD FLOOR
HOBOKEN, NJ 07030

WWW.MHPBOOKS.COM

SECOND MELVILLE HOUSE PRINTING: JANUARY 2008
ISBN: 978-0-976140-72-6

LIBRARY OF CONGRESS CATALOGING-IN-PUBLICATION DATA

Kleist, Heinrich von, 1777-1811.
  [Michael Kolhaas. English]
  Michael Kohlhaas / by Heinrich von Kleist ; translated by
Martin Greenberg.
      p. cm.
  ISBN 0-9761407-2-1
  I. Greenberg, Martin, 1918 Feb. 3- II. Title.
  PT2378.M62G74 2004
  833'.6—dc22

2005010704

MICHAEL KOHLHAAS:
FROM AN OLD CHRONICLE

Toward the middle of the sixteenth century, there lived on the banks of the Havel a horse dealer by the name of Michael Kohlhaas, the son of a schoolmaster, one of the most upright and at the same time one of the most terrible men of his day. Until his thirtieth year this extraordinary man would have been thought the very model of a good citizen. In a village that still bears his name, he owned a farm on which he quietly earned a living by his trade; the children with whom his wife presented him were brought up in the fear of God to be industrious and honest; there was not one of his neighbors who had not benefited from his benevolence or his fair-mindedness—the world, in short, would have had every reason to bless his memory, if he had not carried one virtue to excess. But his sense of justice turned him into a brigand and a murderer.

He rode abroad one day with a string of young horses, all fat and glossy-coated, and was turning over in his mind how he would use the profit he hoped to make on them at the fairs—part of it, like the good manager he was, to get new profits, but part, too, for present enjoyment—when he reached the Elbe, and near an imposing castle standing in Saxon territory he came upon a toll gate that he had never found on that road before. He halted his horses just when a heavy shower of rain was coming down and shouted for the tollkeeper, who after a while showed his surly face at the window. The horse dealer told him to open the gate. "What's been happening here?" he asked, when the tollkeeper, after a long interval, emerged from the house.

"Seigniorial privilege," answered the latter as he opened the gate, "bestowed upon the Junker Wenzel von Tronka."

"So," said Kohlhaas; "the Junker's name is Wenzel?" and he gazed at the castle, which overlooked the field with its glittering battlements. "Is the old Junker dead then?"

"Died of a stroke," the tollkeeper said as he raised the toll bar.

"Oh! I'm sorry to hear that," Kohlhaas replied. "He was a decent old gentleman, who liked to see people come and go and helped along trade and traffic whenever he could; he once put down some cobblestones because a mare of mine broke her leg over there where the road goes into the village. Well, what do I owe you?" he asked, and had trouble getting out the groschen demanded by the keeper from beneath his cloak which was flapping in the wind. "All right, old fellow," he added, when the keeper muttered "Quick, quick!" and cursed the weather; "If they had left this tree standing in the forest it would have been better for both of us." And he gave him the money and started to ride on. He had hardly passed under the toll bar, however, when a new voice rang out from the tower behind him: "Hold up there, horse dealer!" and he saw the castellan slam a window shut and come hurrying down to him. "Now what?" wondered Kohlhaas and halted with his horses. Buttoning one waist-coat after another around his ample middle, the castellan came up to him and, leaning into the wind, asked for his pass.

"Pass?" said Kohlhaas, a little disconcerted. So far as he knew, he had none, was his answer, but if somebody would only tell him what in the name of God the thing was, he might just happen to have one in his pocket. The castellan eyed him obliquely and said that without a permit from the sovereign no dealer could bring horses across the border. The horse dealer assured him that he had already crossed the border seventeen times in his life without such a permit; that he knew every one of the regulations of his trade; that in all likelihood the whole thing would turn out to be a mistake, for which reason he wished to give it some thought; and that he would like it, since he had a long day's ride ahead of him, if he were not needlessly detained any longer. But the castellan answered that he was not going to slip through the eighteenth time, that the ordinance had recently been issued for just that reason, and that he must either get a permit for himself right now or go back to where he had come from. After a moment's reflection, the horse dealer, whom these illegal demands were beginning to exasperate, got down from his horse, handed the reins to a groom, and said that he would speak to the Junker von Tronka himself about the matter. He made straight for the castle, too; the castellan, muttering something about penny-pinching money-grubbers and what a good thing it was to squeeze them, followed him; and the two men, measuring each other with their glances, entered the hall. The Junker happened to be making merry with friends over wine, and they had all burst into uproarious laughter at a joke just as Kohlhaas approached with his complaint. The Junker asked him what he wanted; the knights, on catching sight of the stranger, fell silent; but no sooner did the latter launch into his request about the horses than the whole company cried out, "Horses! Where are they?" and ran to the window. Seeing the shiny-coated string below, they followed the suggestion of the Junker and trooped down into the courtyard; the rain had stopped; castellan, steward, and grooms gathered around them, and the entire yard looked the horses over. One knight praised the bay with the white blaze on his forehead, another liked the chestnut, a third patted the piebald with the tawny spot; and all thought that the horses were like deer and that no finer ones were raised in the country.

Kohlhaas cheerfully replied that the horses were no better than the knights who were going to ride them, and invited them to buy. The Junker, who was very tempted by the big bay stallion, went so far as to ask its price; his steward urged him to buy a pair of blacks that he thought they could use in the fields, since they were short of horses; but when the horse dealer named his price, the knights thought it too dear, and the Junker said that Kohlhaas would have to ride to the Round Table and look for King Arthur if that was the kind of money he wanted for his stock. Kohlhaas, noticing the castellan and the steward whispering together while they shot meaningful looks at the blacks, and moved by a dark presentiment, did everything in his power to sell the horses. He said to the Junker, "Sir, I bought those blacks there six months ago for twenty-five gold gulden; give me thirty and they are yours." Two of the knights standing next to the Junker remarked quite audibly that the horses were probably worth that much; the Junker, however, felt that he might be willing to pay money for the bay but not for the blacks, and he got ready to go back into the castle; whereupon Kohlhaas said that the next time he came that way with his animals they might perhaps strike a bargain, took leave of the Junker, and, gathering up the reins of his horse, started to ride off. But just then the castellan stepped out of the crowd and said it was his understanding that he could not travel without a pass. Kohlhaas turned and asked the Junker if there actually were such a requirement, which would mean the ruin of his whole trade. The Junker, as he walked away, replied with an embarrassed air, "Yes, Kohlhaas, I'm afraid you must have a pass. Speak to the castellan about it and go on your way." Kohlhaas assured him that he had not the least intention of evading whatever regulations there might be for the export of horses; promised that when he went through Dresden he would take out a permit at the privy chancellery; and asked to be allowed to go through just this once since he had known nothing at all about the requirement. "Oh well," said the Junker as the wind began to blow again and whistled between his skinny legs, "let the poor wretch go on. Come!" he said to the knights, turned, and started toward the castle. The castellan, turning to the Junker, said that Kohlhaas at least should leave a pledge behind as security for his taking out the permit. The Junker stopped again inside the castle gate. Kohlhaas asked the amount of security, in money or in articles, that he would have to leave in pledge for the blacks. The steward muttered in his beard that he might just as well leave the blacks themselves. "Of course," said the castellan. "That's just the thing; as soon as he has the pass he can come and fetch his horses whenever he pleases." Taken aback by such a shameless demand, Kohlhaas told the Junker, who was wrapping the skirts of his doublet about his shivering body, that what he wanted to do was to sell the blacks; but just then a gust of wind blew a splatter of rain and hail through the gate and the Junker, to put an end to the business, called out, "If he won't give up the horses, just throw him back over the toll bar," and he went in. The horse dealer, seeing that he had no choice but to yield, decided to give in to the demand; stripping the blacks of their harness, he led them into a stable that the castellan pointed out to him. He left a groom behind with them, gave him some money, and warned him to take good care of the horses until his return; and, uncertain in his own mind whether such a law might not after all have been passed in Saxony to protect the infant occupation of horse breeding, Kohlhaas continued his journey to Leipzig, where he intended to visit the fair, with the rest of the string.

Arriving in Dresden, in one of whose suburbs he owned a house and stables that served him as headquarters for the business he did at the smaller fairs around the country, he went immediately to the chancellery, where he learned from the councilors, some of whom he knew personally, that, just as he had first suspected, the story about the pass was a fable. Kohlhaas, whom the displeased councilors provided with the written certificate he asked of them, testifying to the fact that there was no such regulation, smiled to himself at the skinny Junker's joke, although he could not for the life of him see what the point of it was; and a few weeks later, having satisfactorily disposed of his horses, he returned to Tronka Castle with no more bitterness in his heart than was inspired by the ordinary distress of the world.

The castellan made no comment on the certificate when Kohlhaas showed it to him and told the horse dealer, who asked him if he could now have his horses back, that he only needed to go down to the stables and get them. But Kohlhaas learned with dismay, even while crossing the yard, that his groom had been thrashed for his insolence, as it was called, a few days after being left behind at the castle and had been driven away. He asked the boy who gave him this news what the groom had done, and who had taken care of the horses in the meantime, but the boy said he did not know and, turning from the horse dealer, whose heart was already swollen with misgivings, he opened the stable door. Nevertheless, the horse dealer was shocked when instead of his two sleek, well-fed blacks he saw a pair of scrawny, worn-out nags: ribs like rails on which objects could have been hung, manes and coats matted from lack of care and attention—the very image of misery in the animal kingdom! Kohlhaas, at the sight of whom the beasts neighed and stirred feebly, was beside himself, and demanded to know what had happened to his animals. The boy answered that they had not suffered any harm and that they had had proper feed, too, but since it had been harvest time and there was a shortage of draft animals, they had been used a bit in the fields. Kohlhaas cursed the shameful, deliberate outrage, but, feeling how helpless he was, he stifled his fury and was getting ready to leave the robbers' nest with his horses again—for there was nothing else he could do—when the castellan, attracted by the sound of voices, appeared and asked him what the matter was.

"What's the matter!" Kohlhaas shot out. "Who gave the Junker von Tronka and his people permission to put the blacks I left here to work in the fields?" He asked if that was a decent thing to do, tried to rouse the exhausted beasts with a flick of his whip, and showed him that they did not move. The castellan, after looking at him contemptuously for a while, retorted, "Look at the brute! Shouldn't the clown thank God just to find his nags are still alive?" He asked who was expected to take care of them after the groom had run away, and if it was not right for the horses to pay for their feed by working in the fields. He ended by saying that Kohlhaas had better not try to start anything or he would call the dogs and restore order in the yard that way.

The horse dealer's heart thumped against his doublet. He wanted to pitch the good-for-nothing tub of guts into the mud and grind his heel into his copper-colored face. But his sense of justice, which was as delicate as a gold balance, still wavered; he could not be sure, before the bar of his own conscience, whether the man was really guilty of a crime; and so, swallowing his curses, he went over to the horses and silently weighed all the circumstances while unknotting their manes, then asked in a subdued voice: What was the reason for the groom's having been turned out of the castle? The castellan replied, "Because the rascal was insolent in the stable yard! Because he tried to stand in the way of a change we needed to make in the stabling and wanted us to put the mounts of two young gentlemen who came to the castle out on the

high road overnight for the sake of his own two nags!"
Kohlhaas would have given as much as the horses
were worth to have had the groom right there so as to
compare his account of things with that of the thick-
lipped castellan. He was still standing there, combing
the tangles out of the blacks' manes with his fingers
and wondering what to do next, when the scene suddenly changed and the Junker Wenzel von Tronka,
coming home from coursing hares, galloped into the
castle yard at the head of a troop of knights, grooms,
and dogs. The castellan, when the Junker asked him
what had happened, started right in, with the dogs'
howling murderously from one side on their catching
sight of the stranger and the knights' shouting them
down from the other, to give the Junker a viciously
distorted account of the uproar the horse dealer was
making just because his pair of blacks had been exer-
cised a bit. With a scornful laugh he said that the
horse dealer even refused to recognize the horses as
his own. Kohlhaas cried out, "Those are not my horses, your worship! Those are not the horses which were
worth thirty gold gulden! I want my well fed and
healthy horses back!"

The Junker, whose face paled for a moment,
dismounted and said, "If the son of a bitch won't take
his horses back, he can let things stay just as they are.
Come, Günther!" he cried, "Hans, come!" while he
beat the dust from his breeches with his hand; as he
passed under the gate with the knights, he again cried,
"Fetch some wine!" and entered the castle. Kohlhaas

said he would rather call the knacker and have his horses thrown into the carrion pit than bring them back the way they were to his stables at Kohlhaasenbrück. Turning his back on the animals and leaving them where they were, he mounted his bay and, swearing he would know how to get justice for himself, rode away.

He was already galloping full tilt down the road to Dresden when the thought of the groom and what they had accused him of at the castle slowed him to a walk and, before he had gone a thousand paces, he turned his horse around and headed for Kohlhaasenbrück, intending, as seemed right and prudent to him, to hear the groom's side of the story first. For in spite of the humiliations he had suffered, a correct feeling, based on what he already knew about the imperfect state of the world, made him inclined, in case the groom were at all guilty, as the castellan claimed, to put up with the loss of his horses as being after all a just consequence. But this was disputed by an equally commendable feeling, which took deeper and deeper root the farther he rode and the more he heard at every stop about the injustices perpetrated daily against travelers at Tronka Castle, that, if the whole incident proved to have been premeditated, as seemed probable, it was his duty to the world to do everything in his power to get satisfaction for himself for the wrong done him, and a guarantee against future ones for his fellow citizens.

No sooner had he arrived at Kohlhaasenbrück, embraced his faithful wife Lisbeth, and kissed his children who were shouting with glee around his knees, than he asked after Herse the head groom: Had anything been heard from him? "Oh yes, Michael dear," Lisbeth answered, "that Herse! Just imagine, the poor man turned up here about a fortnight ago, terribly beaten and bruised; so beaten, in fact, that he can't even draw a full breath. We put him to bed, where he kept coughing up blood, and after we asked him over and over again what had happened he told us a story that nobody understands. How you left him behind at Tronka Castle in charge of some horses they wouldn't let pass through there; how they had mistreated him shamefully and forced him to leave the castle; and how it had been impossible for him to bring the horses with him."

"So?" said Kohlhaas, taking off his cloak. "I suppose he is all recovered now?"

"Pretty well, except for his coughing blood. I wanted to send a groom to Tronka Castle right away to look after the horses until you got back there. Since Herse has always been an honest servant to us—in fact, more loyal than anybody else—I felt I had no right to doubt his story, especially when he had so many bruises to confirm it, and to suspect him of losing the horses in some other way. But he pleaded with me not to expect anybody to venture into that den of thieves, and to give the animals up if I didn't want to sacrifice a man's life for them."

"Is he still in bed?" asked Kohlhaas, taking off his neckerchief.

"He has been walking around the yard again," she said, "these last few days. But you will see for yourself," she went on, "that it's all quite true, and that it is another one of those outrages against strangers they have been allowing themselves lately up at Tronka Castle."

"Well, I'll have to investigate the business first," Kohlhaas replied. "Would you call him in here, Lisbeth, if he is up and around?" With these words he lowered himself into an armchair while his wife, who was delighted to see him taking things so calmly, went to fetch the groom.

"What have you been doing at Tronka Castle?" asked Kohlhaas when Herse followed Lisbeth into the room. "I can't say that I am too pleased with your conduct."

The groom's pale face showed spots of red at these words, and he was silent for a moment. Then he said, "You are quite right, sir. When I heard a child crying inside the castle, I threw a sulphur match into the Elbe that Providence had put in my pocket to burn down that robbers' nest I was chased out of, and I thought to myself: Let God lay it in ashes with one of his lightning bolts, I won't!"

Kohlhaas was taken aback. "But how did you manage to get yourself chased out of the castle?" he asked.

"They played me a nasty trick, sir," Herse replied, wiping the sweat from his forehead. "But what's done is done and can't be undone. I wouldn't let them work the horses to death in the fields, so I said they were still young and had never really been in harness."

Kohlhaas, trying to hide his confusion, replied that Herse had not told the exact truth, since the horses had been in harness for a little while at the beginning of the past spring. "As you were a sort of guest at the castle," he continued, "you really might have obliged them once or twice when they needed help to bring the harvest in faster."

"But I did do that, sir," Herse said. "I thought that, as long as they were giving me such nasty looks, it wouldn't, after all, lose me the blacks, and so on the third morning I hitched them up and brought in three wagonloads of grain."

Kohlhaas, whose heart began to swell, looked down at the ground and said, "They didn't say a word about that, Herse!"

Herse swore it was so. "How was I rude?—I didn't want to yoke the horses up again when they had hardly finished their midday feeding; and when the castellan and the steward offered me free fodder if I would do it, so I could put the money you had given me for feed in my own pocket, I told them I would do something they hadn't bargained for: I turned around and walked off."

"But surely you weren't driven away from the castle for that?" said Kohlhaas.

"Mercy, no," cried the groom. "For a very wicked crime indeed! That evening the mounts of two knights who came to Tronka Castle were led into the stable and my horses were tied to the stable door. When I took the blacks from the castellan, who was taking care of the quartering himself, and asked him where my animals were to go now, he pointed to a pigsty knocked together out of laths and boards that was leaning against the castle wall."

"You mean," interrupted Kohlhaas, "that it was such a sorry shelter for horses that it was more like a pigsty than a stable?"

"It was a pigsty, sir," Herse replied, "really and truly a pigsty, with pigs running in and out; I couldn't stand up straight in it."

"Perhaps there was no other shelter for the blacks," Kohlhaas said. "In a way, the knights' horses had first call."

"There wasn't much room," the groom answered, letting his voice sink. "All told, there were seven knights at the castle. If it had been you, you would have had the horses moved a little closer together. I said I would look for a stable to rent in the village; but the castellan replied that he had to keep the horses under his own eyes and that I wasn't to dare take them out of the yard."

"Hm!" said Kohlhaas. "What did you say to that?"

"Since the steward said the two visitors would only be staying overnight and would be riding on the next morning, I put the horses into the pigsty. But the next day came and went without their making a move; and on the third day I heard that the gentlemen were going to stay some weeks longer at the castle."

"Well, after all, Herse," said Kohlhaas, "it wasn't as bad in the pigsty as it seemed to you when you first poked your nose into it."

"That's true," the groom answered. "After I had swept the place out a little, it wasn't so bad. I gave the girl a groschen to put her pigs somewhere else. And by taking the roof boards off at dawn and laying them on again at night, I arranged it so that the horses could stand upright during the day. So there they stood, their heads poking out of the roof like geese in a coop, and looked around for Kohlhaasenbrück or wherever life was better."

"Well then," Kohlhaas said, "why in the world did they drive you away?"

"Sir, I'll tell you," the groom replied. "Because they wanted to get rid of me. Because, as long as I was there, they couldn't work the horses to death. In the yard, in the servants' hall, everywhere, they made ugly faces at me; and because I thought to myself, 'You can pull your jaws down till you dislocate them, for all I care,' they picked a quarrel and threw me out."

"But the pretext!" cried Kohlhaas. "They must have had some pretext!"

"Oh of course," answered Herse, "the best imaginable! The second day after we had moved into the pigsty, that evening I took the horses, which had got mucky in spite of everything, and started to ride them over to the horse pond. Just as I was passing through the castle gate and began to turn off, I heard the castellan and the steward clattering after me out of the servants' hall with men, dogs, and sticks, shouting, 'Stop thief! Catch the rogue!' as if they were possessed. The gatekeeper blocked my way; and when I asked him and the wild mob running after me, 'What the devil's the matter?'—'What's the matter!' answered the castellan, and he caught my two blacks by the bridle. 'Where do you think you are going with those horses?' he asked, grabbing me by the front of my shirt. 'Where am I going?' I said. 'Thunder and lightning! I'm riding over to the horse pond. Did you think I—?'—'To the horse pond!' the castellan shouted. 'I'll teach you, you rogue, to go swimming along the high road to Kohlhaasenbrück!' And with a vicious jerk he and the steward, who had caught me by the leg, flung me down from the horse so that I measured my full length in the mud. 'Murder!' I cried. 'There are breast straps and blankets and a bundle of laundry belonging to me in the stable!' But while the steward led the horses away, he and the grooms jumped on me with feet and whips and clubs, leaving me half dead on the ground outside the castle gate. When I cried, 'The robbers! Where are they going with my horses?' and got to my feet, the castellan screamed, 'Out of the castle yard, you! Sick him, Caesar! Sick him, Hunter! Sick him, Spitz!' And a pack of more than twelve dogs rushed at me. Then I tore something from the fence, a picket maybe, I can't remember, and stretched out three dogs dead on the ground at my feet; but just when I had to fall back because of the terrible bites I had gotten, there was a shrill whistle: 'Whee—oo!' the dogs scurried back to the yard, the gate slammed shut, the bolt shot home, and I fell down unconscious on the road."

Kohlhaas, white in the face, said with forced shrewdness, "Didn't you really want to escape, Herse?" And when the latter, with a deep blush, stared at the ground, the horse dealer said, "Confess it! You didn't like it one bit in the pigsty; you thought to yourself how much better it was, after all, in the stable at Kohlhaasenbrück."

"Thunder!" cried Herse. "Breast strap and blankets I left behind in the pigsty, and a bundle of laundry, I tell you! Wouldn't I have taken along the three gulden I wrapped in a red silk neck cloth and hid behind the manger? Blazes, hell, and the devil! When you talk like that, I feel again like lighting that sulphur match I threw away!"

"All right, never mind," said the horse dealer. "There was no harm meant, really. Look, I believe every word you've told me; and if the matter ever comes up, I am ready to take holy communion myself on the truth of what you say. I am sorry things haven't gone better for you in my service. Go back to bed now, Herse, won't you, let them bring you a bottle of wine, and console yourself: Justice shall be done you!" And he stood up, jotted down a list of the things the head groom had left behind in the pigsty, noted the value of each, also asked him what he estimated the cost of his doctoring at, and, after shaking hands with him once more, dismissed him.

Then he told Lisbeth, his wife, the full story of what had happened, explained its meaning, said his mind was made up to seek justice at the law, and had the satisfaction of seeing that she supported his purpose heart and soul. For she said that many other travelers, perhaps less patient ones than himself, would pass by that castle; that it was doing God's work to put a stop to such disorders; and that she would manage to get together the money he needed to pay the expenses of the lawsuit. Kohlhaas called her his brave wife, spent that day and the next very happily with her and the children and, as soon as his business permitted, set out for Dresden to lay his complaint before the court.

There, with the help of a lawyer he knew, he drew up a list of charges which described in detail the outrage the Junker Wenzel von Tronka had committed against him and his groom Herse, and which petitioned the court to punish the knight according to the law, to restore his, Kohlhaas', horses to him in their original condition, and to have him and his groom compensated for the damages they had sustained. His case seemed an open-and-shut one. The fact that his horses had been illegally detained pretty well decided everything else; and even if one supposed that they had taken sick by sheer accident, the horse dealer's demand that they should be returned to him in sound condition would still have been a just one. Nor did Kohlhaas, as he looked about the capital, lack for friends who promised to give his case their active support; the large trade he did in horses had made him acquainted with the most important men of the country, and his honest dealing had won him their good will. He dined cheerfully a number of times with his lawyer, who was himself a man of consequence; left a sum of money with him to defray the legal costs; and, fully reassured by the latter as to the outcome of the suit, returned, in a few weeks' time, to his wife Lisbeth in Kohlhaasenbrück. Yet months passed and the year was nearing its close before he even received an official notice from Saxony about the suit he had instituted there, let alone any final decision. After he had petitioned the court several more times, he sent a confidential letter to his lawyer asking what was responsible for the excessive delay, and learned that the Dresden court, upon the intervention of an influential person, had dismissed his suit out of hand.

When the horse dealer wrote back in astonishment, asking what the explanation for this was, the lawyer reported that the Junker Wenzel von Tronka was related to two young noblemen, Hinz and Kunz von Tronka, one of whom was Cupbearer to the sovereign's person, and the other actually Chamberlain. He advised Kohlhaas to waste no more time on the court, but to go to Tronka Castle where the horses still were and try to get them back himself; gave him to understand that the Junker, who was just then stopping in the capital, had apparently left orders with his people to turn them over to him; and closed with a request to be excused from acting any further in the matter in case Kohlhaas was still not satisfied.

The horse dealer happened to be in Brandenburg at this time, where the Governor of the city, Heinrich von Geusau, within whose jurisdiction Kohlhaasenbrück lay, was just then occupied in setting up a number of charitable institutions for the sick and the poor, out of a considerable fund that had come to the city. He was especially concerned with roofing over and enclosing a mineral spring for the use of invalids, which was located in one of the nearby villages and which was thought to have greater healing powers than it subsequently proved to possess; and as Kohlhaas had transacted a good deal of business with him during his stay at court and therefore was acquainted with him, the Governor allowed Herse, who ever since those unhappy days at Tronka Castle had suffered from pains in the chest when breathing, to try the curative effects of the little spring. It so happened that the Governor was present at the edge of the basin in which Kohlhaas had placed Herse, giving certain directions, just when a messenger from Lisbeth put into the horse dealer's hands the discouraging letter from his lawyer in Dresden. The Governor, while he was talking to the doctor, noticed Kohlhaas drop a tear on the letter he had received and read; he walked over to Kohlhaas with friendly sympathy and asked him what the bad news was; and when the horse dealer said nothing but handed him the letter, the worthy gentleman clapped him on the shoulder, for he knew the outrageous wrong done Kohlhaas at Tronka Castle as a result of which Herse lay sick right there, perhaps for the rest of his life, and told him not to be discouraged, he would help him to get satisfaction! That evening, when the horse dealer waited upon him in his castle as he had been bidden, he advised him that all he had to do was to draw up a petition to the Elector of Brandenburg briefly describing the incident, enclose the lawyer's letter, and solicit, on account of the violence done him on Saxon territory, the protection of the sovereign. He promised to include the petition in another packet that he was just sending to the Elector, who, if circumstances at all permitted, would unfailingly intervene on his behalf with the Elector of Saxony; and nothing more than this was needed to obtain justice for Kohlhaas from the Dresden court, in spite of all the tricks of the Junker and his henchmen. Overjoyed, Kohlhaas thanked the Governor earnestly for this fresh proof of his good will; said he was only sorry he had not begun proceedings in Berlin right off, without bothering with Dresden; and after duly drawing up the complaint at the chancellery of the municipal court and delivering it to the Governor, he returned to Kohlhaasenbrück feeling more confident than ever before about the outcome of his case. But only a few weeks later he was troubled to learn, from a magistrate who was going to Potsdam on business for the City Governor, that the Elector of Brandenburg had turned the petition over to his Chancellor, Count Kallheim, and the latter, instead of directly requesting the Dresden court to investigate the outrage and punish the culprits, as would have seemed the appropriate course, had first, as a preliminary step, applied to the Junker von Tronka for further information. The magistrate, who stopped in his carriage outside Kohlhaas' house, had apparently been instructed to deliver this message to the horse dealer, but he could not satisfactorily answer the latter's anxious question as to why such a procedure was being followed. He added only that the Governor sent Kohlhaas word to be patient; he seemed in a hurry to be on his way; and not until the very end of the short interview did the horse dealer gather from some remarks he let fall that Count Kallheim was connected by marriage with the house of Tronka.

Kohlhaas, who could no longer take any pleasure either in his horse breeding or his house and farm, hardly even in his wife and children, waited with gloomy forebodings for the new month; and, just as he had expected, Herse came back from Brandenburg at the end of this time, his health a little better for the baths, bringing a rather lengthy resolution accompanied by a letter from the City Governor that said: He was sorry he could do nothing about his case for him; he was sending along a resolution of the Chancery of State that was meant for Kohlhaas; and his advice to him was to go and fetch the horses he had left at Tronka Castle and forget about everything else. The resolution read as follows: that according to the Dresden court report, he was an idle, quarrelsome fellow; the Junker with whom he had left his horses was not keeping them from him in any way; let him send to the castle and take them away, or at least inform the Junker where to send them to him; in any case, he was not to trouble the Chancery of State with such petty quarrels. Kohlhaas, who cared nothing about the horses themselves—his pain would have been just as great if it had been a question of a pair of dogs—was consumed with rage when he received this letter. Every time he heard a noise in the yard, he looked toward the gate, with the unpleasantest feelings of anticipation that had ever stirred in his breast, to see whether the Junker's men had come to give him back, perhaps even with an apology, his starved and worn-out horses—the only instance in which his soul, well-disciplined though it was by the world, was utterly unprepared for something it fully expected to happen. A short time after, however, he learned from an acquaintance, who had traveled the high-road, that his animals were still being worked in the fields at Tronka Castle, now as before, just like the Junker's other horses; and through the pain he felt at seeing the world in such a state of monstrous disorder flashed a thrill of inward satisfaction at knowing that henceforth he would be at peace with himself.

He invited a bailiff, who was his neighbor and who for a long time had had the plan of enlarging his estate by buying property adjoining it, to come and see him and asked him, after the visitor was seated, how much he would give him for all the property Kohlhaas owned in Brandenburg and Saxony, house and farm, immovable or otherwise, the whole lot of it together. His wife, Lisbeth, turned pale at these words. Turning around and picking up her youngest child who was playing on the floor behind her, she shot a deathly glance past the red cheeks of the little boy, who was tugging at her neckerchief, at the horse dealer and the sheet of paper in his hand. The bailiff stared at him in surprise and asked what had put such a strange notion into his head all of a sudden; to which the horse dealer replied, with as much cheerfulness as he could muster: that the idea of selling his farm on the banks of the Havel was not, after all, an entirely new one; the two of them had often discussed the matter together in the past; his house in the outskirts of Dresden was, in comparison with it, just something thrown in that they could forget about; in short, if the bailiff would do as he wished him to and take over both pieces of property, he was ready to close the contract with him. He added, with rather forced humor, that Kohlhaasenbrück was, after all, not the world; there might be purposes in life compared to which that of being a good father to his family was an inferior and unworthy one; in short, he must tell him that his soul aimed at great things, about which he would perhaps be hearing shortly. The bailiff, reassured by these words, said jokingly to Kohlhaas' wife, who was kissing her child over and over again, "Surely he won't insist on being paid right away!" laid his hat and stick which he had been holding between his knees on the table, and took the sheet of paper from the horse dealer's hand to read it over. Kohlhaas, moving his chair closer to him, explained that it was a contingent bill of sale that he had drawn up himself, with a four-weeks' right of cancellation; showed him how nothing was lacking but their signatures and the insertion of the actual purchase price, as well as the amount of forfeit Kohlhaas would agree to pay in case he withdrew from the contract within the four-weeks' period; and again urged the bailiff good-humoredly to make an offer, assuring him that he would be reasonable as to the amount and easy as to the terms. His wife marched up and down the room, her bosom heaving with such violence that the kerchief at which the boy had been tugging threatened to come off her shoulders. The bailiff observed that he really had no way of judging how much the Dresden property was worth; whereupon Kohlhaas pushed some letters over to him that he had exchanged with the seller at the time of purchase, and answered that he put it at one hundred gold gulden, though the letters would show that it had cost him almost half as much again. The bailiff reread the bill of sale and found that it gave him the unusual right, as buyer, to withdraw from the contract, too, and he said, with his mind already half made up, that of course he would not have any use for the stud horses in his stables; when Kohlhaas replied that he had no intention of parting with the horses, nor with some weapons hanging in the armory, the bailiff hemmed and hawed and at last he repeated an offer—a paltry one indeed, considering the value of the property—that he had made him once before, half in jest and half in earnest, when they were out walking together. Kohlhaas pushed pen and ink over for him to sign. The bailiff, who could not believe his senses, again asked him if he were serious; when the horse dealer answered, a little testily: Did he think he was only joking with him, the former, with a very serious face, finally took up the pen and signed; however, he crossed out the clause concerning the forfeit payable by the seller if he should withdraw from the bargain; promised to lend Kohlhaas one hundred gold gulden against a mortgage on the Dresden property, which he absolutely refused to buy from him; and said that Kohlhaas was perfectly free to change his mind at any time within the next two months. The horse dealer, touched by his behavior, warmly shook his hand; and after they had agreed to a main stipulation, which was that a fourth part of the purchase price should be paid immediately in cash and the balance into the Hamburg bank in three months' time, Kohlhaas called for wine in order to celebrate the happy conclusion of their bargain. When the maidservant entered with the wine bottles, he asked her to tell Sternbald, the groom, to saddle his chestnut horse; he meant, he announced, to ride to the capital, where he had some business to attend to; and he let it be understood that in a short time, after he had returned, he would be able to talk more frankly about what, for the present, he must keep to himself. Then, pouring out the wine, he asked about the Poles and the Turks who were just then at war; engaged the bailiff in all sorts of political conjectures on the subject; drank once more to the success of their business; and showed the bailiff to the door.

When the bailiff had left the room, Lisbeth fell on her knees in front of her husband. "If you have any affection for me," she cried, "for me and for the children I have borne you, if you haven't already cast us out of your heart, for what reason I don't know, then tell me what the meaning of all this is!"

"Nothing, my dear wife," said Kohlhaas, "that you need to get upset about, as matters stand at present. I have received a resolution in which I am told that my complaint against the Junker Wenzel von Tronka is mere quarrelsomeness and mischief-making. And as there must be some misunderstanding here, I have decided to present my complaint again, in person, to the sovereign himself."

"But why do you want to sell your house?" she cried, rising with a gesture of despair.

The horse dealer took her gently in his arms and said, "Because, dearest Lisbeth, I will not go on living in a country where they won't protect me in my rights. I'd rather be a dog, if people are going to kick me, than a man! I am sure my wife thinks about this just as I do."

"How do you know," she asked him in a gentle voice, "that they won't protect you in your rights? If you go to the Elector humbly with your petition, as it is proper that you should, how do you know that it will be tossed aside or that his answer will be to refuse you a hearing?"

"Very well," Kohlhaas said, "if my fears are groundless, neither has my house been sold yet. The Elector himself, I know, is a just man; and if I can only slip past those around him and speak to his own person, I don't doubt that I shall get justice for myself and come happily home again to you and my old trade before the week is out. And then I should only want to stay with you," he added, kissing her, "till the end of my life! However," he continued, "it is best for me to be prepared for everything; and therefore I should like you, if possible, to go away for a while with the children and visit your aunt in Schwerin, whom you have been wanting to visit for some time anyhow."

"What!" exclaimed his wife. "I'm to go to Schwerin? Across the border with the children to my aunt in Schwerin?" And terror made the words stick in her throat.

"Certainly," Kohlhaas said. "And, if possible, right away, since I don't want to be worrying about other things while I am busy with the steps I mean to take in my case."

"Oh, now I understand you!" she exclaimed. "All you want now are arms and horses, whoever wants the rest can have it!" And she turned away from him, threw herself into a chair, and burst into tears.

"Dearest Lisbeth," Kohlhaas said in surprise, "what are you saying? I have been blessed by God with wife and children and worldly goods; am I to wish it were otherwise for the first time today?" He sat down next to her when she flushed at these words, and she threw her arms around his neck. "Tell me," he said, smoothing the hair away from her forehead, "what shall I do? Shall I give up my suit? Shall I go over to Tronka Castle, beg the knight to give me back my horses, and mount and ride them home to you?"

Lisbeth did not dare to say, "Yes! Yes! Yes!"—weeping, she shook her head, hugged him fiercely to her, and covered his breast with fervent kisses.

"Well then," Kohlhaas cried, "if you feel that justice must be done me if I am to continue in my trade, then don't deny me the freedom I need to get it!" And, standing up, he ordered the groom, who had come to report that the chestnut was saddled and ready, to see to it that the bays were harnessed the next day to take his wife to Schwerin. Lisbeth said she had just thought of something. Rising and wiping the tears from her eyes, she asked her husband, who had sat down at his desk, if he would entrust the petition to her and let her go to Berlin in his stead and hand it to the Elector. Kohlhaas, moved by this change in her for more reasons than one, drew her down on his lap and said, "My darling wife, that is hardly possible. The sovereign is surrounded by a great many people, anybody coming near him is exposed to all sorts of annoyances."

Lisbeth replied that in nine cases out of ten it was easier for a woman to approach him than a man. "Give me the petition," she repeated, "and if all you want is an assurance that it will reach his hands, I guarantee he'll receive it!" Kohlhaas, who had had many proofs of her courage as well as her intelligence, asked her how she proposed to go about it; whereupon, looking shamefacedly at the ground, she answered that the castellan of the Elector's palace had courted her in earlier days, when he had served in Schwerin; that it was true he was married now and the father of several children, but that she was still not entirely forgotten— in short, let him leave it to her to make use of this as well as many other circumstances, which it would take too long to describe. Kohlhaas kissed her happily, said that her proposal was accepted, advised her that all she needed to do to speak to the sovereign inside the palace itself was to lodge with the wife of the castellan, gave her the petition, ordered the bays harnessed up, and, bundling her into the wagon, sent her off with his faithful groom, Sternbald.

But of all the unsuccessful steps that he had taken in his case, this journey was the most unfortunate. For only a few days later Sternbald entered the courtyard again, leading the wagon at a walk, inside of which the horse dealer's wife lay prostrate with a dangerous contusion of the chest. Kohlhaas, white-faced, came running over, but could get no coherent account of the cause of the accident. The castellan, according to the groom, had not been at home, so they had had to put up at an inn near the palace; Lisbeth had left the inn the next morning, ordering the groom to remain with the horses; and she had not returned until evening, in her present condition. Apparently she had pressed forward too boldly toward the sovereign's person and, through no fault of his, only because of the brutal zeal of a bodyguard, she had received a blow on the chest from a lance butt. At least that was what the people had said who brought her back unconscious to the inn toward evening; for she herself could hardly speak because of the blood flowing from her mouth. Afterwards a knight came to get the petition from her. Sternbald said he had wanted to jump on a horse and gallop home immediately with the news of the accident; but in spite of all the remonstrances of the surgeon called in to attend her, she had insisted on being carried back to her husband at Kohlhaasenbrück without sending word ahead. Kohlhaas found her more dead than alive from the trip, and put her to bed where, gasping painfully for breath, she lived a few days longer. They tried in vain to bring her back to consciousness so as to get some light on what had happened; she lay in bed staring straight in front of her, her eyes already dim, and would not answer. Only just before her death did she recover consciousness. For when a minister of the Lutheran faith (which, following the example of her husband, she had embraced in what was then its infancy) was standing beside her bed, reading, in a loud voice which mixed pathos and solemnity, a chapter of the Bible, she suddenly looked darkly up at him, took the Bible from his hand as if there were no need to read to her from it, turned page after page, apparently looking for a passage; then her forefinger pointed out this verse to Kohlhaas, who was sitting at her bedside: "Forgive your enemies; do good to them that hate you." As she did so, she squeezed his hand with a look full of tender feeling, and died.

Kohlhaas thought: "May God never forgive me the way I forgive the Junker!" kissed her with the tears streaming down his cheeks, closed her eyes, and left the room. Taking the hundred gold gulden that the bailiff had already sent him for the stables in Dresden, he ordered such a funeral as became a princess better than a horse dealer's wife: an oak coffin with heavy brass mountings, cushions of silk with gold and silver tassels, and a grave eight ells deep, walled with fieldstone and mortar. He himself stood beside the tomb with his youngest child in his arms and looked on at the work. On the day of the funeral the corpse, white as snow, was laid out in a room that he had had hung with black cloth. The minister had just finished speaking with great feeling at the bier, when the sovereign's answer to the petition presented him by the dead woman was delivered to Kohlhaas: He was commanded to fetch the horses home from Tronka Castle and let the matter drop, on pain of imprisonment. Kohlhaas stuffed the letter in his pocket and had the coffin carried out to the wagon. As soon as the grave mound was raised, a cross planted on it, and the funeral guests gone, he flung himself down once more before his wife's now empty bed, then set about the business of his revenge. He sat down and drew up a decree that, by virtue of the authority inborn in him, commanded the Junker von Tronka, within three days of its receipt, to bring back to Kohlhaasenbrück the pair of blacks he had stolen from him and worked to death in the fields, and to fatten them with his own hands in Kohlhaas's stables. He sent the decree to the Junker by mounted messenger, instructing the man to turn around and come right back to Kohlhaasenbrück as soon as he had delivered it. When the three days passed without the horses being returned, Kohlhaas called over Herse; told him about his ordering the nobleman to fatten the blacks; and asked him two things: Would he ride with him to Tronka Castle and fetch the Junker out; and would he be willing, after they had brought him to Kohlhaasenbrück, to apply the whip to him in the stables in case he should be slow about carrying out the terms of the decree? When Herse, as soon as he understood what was meant, shouted exultantly: "Sir, this very day!" and, throwing his hat in the air, promised that he would plait a thong with ten knots to teach the Junker how to currycomb, Kohlhaas sold the house and sent the children over the border in a wagon; when darkness fell, he called the other grooms together, seven in number, every one of them as true as gold; gave them arms and horses, and set out for Tronka Castle.

With this handful of men, at nightfall of the third day, he attacked the castle, riding down the tollkeeper and gateman as they stood in conversation in the gateway, and while Herse, amid the sudden bursting into flames of all the barracks in the castle yard, raced up the winding stairs of the castle keep and with thrusts and blows fell upon the castellan and the steward, who were sitting half undressed over a game, Kohlhaas dashed into the castle in search of the Junker Wenzel. In such fashion does the angel of judgment descend from heaven. The Junker, who was in the middle of reading aloud the decree sent him by the horse dealer, amid uproarious laughter, to a crowd of young friends staying with him, had no sooner heard the latter's voice in the castle yard than he turned pale as a corpse, cried out, "Brothers, save yourselves!" and vanished. Kohlhaas, entering the hall, grabbed hold of a Junker Hans von Tronka as the latter came at him and flung him into a corner of the room with such force that his brains splattered over the stone floor, and asked, as the other knights, who had drawn their swords, were being routed and over-powered by his men: Where was the Junker Wenzel von Tronka? But, seeing that the stunned men knew nothing, he kicked open the doors of the two rooms leading into the castle wings, searched up and down the rambling structure and, finding no one, went down, cursing, into the castle yard to post guards at the exits. In the meantime, dense clouds of smoke were billowing skywards from the castle and its wings, which had caught fire from the barracks, and, while Stembald and three other men were busy heaping up everything that was not nailed down tight and heaving it out among the horses for plunder, the corpses of the castellan and the steward, with those of their wives and children, came hurtling out of the open windows of the castle keep accompanied by Herse's exultant shouts. Kohlhaas, as he descended the castle stairs, was met by the Junker's gouty old housekeeper who threw herself at his feet; stopping on the stair, he asked her where the Junker Wenzel von Tronka was; and when she answered, in a faint and trembling voice, that she thought he had taken refuge in the chapel, he called over two men with torches, had the door broken down with crowbars and axes (since the keys had vanished), turned altars and benches upside down, and found again, to his furious disappointment, no trace of the Junker. As Kohlhaas emerged from the chapel, he happened to meet a stable boy, one of the castle's servants, running to bring the Junker's chargers out of a large stone stable that was menaced by the flames. Kohlhaas, who that very instant spied his two blacks in a little thatched shed, asked the boy why he did not save them; and when the latter, sticking the key in the stable door, said the shed was already in flames, Kohlhaas snatched the key out of the lock, flung it over the wall, and, raining blows thick as hail on the boy with the flat of his sword, chased him into the burning shed, amid the terrible laughter of the men around him, to save the horses. But when the fellow reappeared, pale with fright, leading the horses in his hand a few moments before the shed collapsed behind him, he found that Kohlhaas had walked away; and when he went over to the grooms in the castle square and asked the horse dealer, who kept turning his back on him, what he should do with the animals now, Kohlhaas suddenly drew his foot back so menacingly that if he had delivered the kick it would have meant his end; mounted his bay without answering him, stationed himself in the castle gate, and in silence waited for daybreak while his men went on with what they were doing. Morning found everything except the

walls of the castle burned to the ground, and not a
soul left in it but Kohlhaas and his seven men. He
dismounted from his horse and in the bright sunlight
that bathed every nook and cranny of the castle yard
he searched the place once more, and when he had to
admit, hard as it was for him, that his attempt on the
castle had failed, with a heart full of pain and grief he
sent out Herse and some grooms to learn in which
direction the Junker had fled. He was especially anxious about a rich nunnery called Erlabrunn that stood
on the banks of the Mulde and whose Abbess,
Antonia von Tronka, was known in the neighborhood
for a pious, charitable, and saintly woman; for it
seemed only too probable to the unhappy Kohlhaas
that the Junker, lacking every necessity as he did, had
taken refuge there, since the Abbess was his own aunt
and had been his instructress in his early years.
Kohlhaas, after informing himself about this circum-
stance, climbed the castle keep, inside of which a
habitable room still remained, and drew up a so-called
"Kohlhaas Manifesto," in which he called upon the
country to give no aid or comfort to the Junker Wenzel
von Tronka, against whom he was waging righteous
war, but instead required every inhabitant, including
relatives and friends, to hand him over forthwith, on
pain of death and the certain destruction by fire of
everything they called their own. He had this manifesto scattered throughout the countryside by travelers and strangers; he even gave a copy of it to his
groom Waldmann, with exact orders about delivering

it into Lady Antonia's hands at Erlabrunn. Then he had a talk with some of the Tronka Castle menials who were dissatisfied with the Junker's service and, drawn by the prospect of plunder, wished to enter his; armed them like foot soldiers with crossbows and daggers and taught them how to ride behind the mounted grooms; and, after turning all the spoils his men had collected into money and dividing it among them, he rested from his sorry labors for an hour or two inside the castle gate.

Toward midday Herse returned and confirmed what Kohlaass' heart, always ready to expect the worst, had already told him: namely, that the Junker was to be found at the convent of Erlabrunn with the old Lady Antonia von Tronka, his aunt. Apparently he had escaped through a door in the castle's back wall and down a narrow, low-roofed stone stairway that led to some boats on the Elbe. At all events, reported Herse, he had turned up at midnight, in a skiff without rudder or oars, in a village on the Elbe—to the astonishment of the inhabitants, whom the burning of Tronka Castle had brought together out of their houses—and had gone on from there to Erlabrunn in a village cart.

Kohlhaas heaved a deep sigh on hearing this; he asked whether the horses had been fed and, on being told yes, he commanded his troop to mount up and in three hours' time stood before Erlabrunn. As he entered the cloister yard with his band, amid the mutterings of a distant storm along the horizon, holding aloft torches he had had lighted outside the place, and his groom Waldmann came up to report that the manifesto had been duly delivered, Kohlhaas perceived the Abbess and the Cloister Warden, in agitated conversation, come out under the portal of the convent; and while the latter, the Warden, a little old man with snow-white hair, shot fierce glances at Kohlhaas as his armor was being strapped on and called out bravely to the servants around him to ring the alarm bell, the former, the Canoness, white as a sheet and holding a silver image of the crucified Christ in her hand, came down the slope and prostrated herself with all her nuns before Kohlhaas' horse. Kohlhaas, as Herse and Sternbald overpowered the Warden, who had no sword, and were leading him off a prisoner among the horses, asked her where the Junker Wenzel von Tronka was, and, when she unfastened a great ring of keys from her girdle and said, "In Wittenberg, good Kohlhaas!" adding in a quavering voice, "Fear God and do no evil!"—the horse dealer, pitched back into the hell of his unslaked thirst for revenge, wheeled his horse and was about to cry, "Set the place on fire!" when a huge lightning bolt struck close beside him. Turning his horse back, Kohlhaas asked her if she had received his manifesto; the lady replied in a faint, barely audible voice, "Just a moment ago!"—"When?"—"Two hours after my nephew, the Junker, departed, so help me God!"—And when Waldmann, the groom, to whom Kohlhaas turned with a lowering glance, stuttered out a confirmation of this, saying that the Mulde's waters, swollen by the rains, had prevented his arriving until a few moments ago, Kohlhaas came to his senses; a sudden fierce downpour of rain, sweeping across the pavement of the yard and extinguishing the torches, loosened the knot of anguish in his unhappy breast; lifting his hat curtly to the Abbess, he wheeled his horse about, dug his spurs in, and crying, "Follow me, brothers, the Junker is in Wittenberg!" he galloped out of the cloister.

When night fell, he halted at an inn on the highroad, where he had to stop a day to rest his weary horses, and as it was clear to him that with a troop of ten—for that was his strength now—he could not challenge so large a place as Wittenberg, he composed a second manifesto, in which he briefly recounted what had happened to him and summoned "all good Christians," as he put it, to whom he "solemnly promised bounty money and other emoluments of war, to take sides with him against the Junker von Tronka as the common enemy of all Christians." In another manifesto, issued shortly after, he called himself "a free gentleman of the Empire and the world, owing allegiance to none but God"—a species of morbid and misdirected fanaticism, for which the clink of his money and the prospect of plunder nevertheless procured him a crowd of recruits from among the rabble whom the peace with Poland had turned out of service: And, in fact, he had some thirty-odd men behind him when he crossed back to the right side of the Elbe with the intention of burning Wittenberg to the ground. Horses and men camped under the roof of a tumble-down brick kiln, in the solitude of a dark woods then surrounding the place, and no sooner had he learned from Sternbald, whom Kohlhaas sent into the city in disguise with the manifesto, that it was already known to the people there, than he rode out with his band on the eve of Whitsuntide and set the city afire at different spots simultaneously while the townspeople lay fast asleep. While his men were plundering the suburbs, Kohlhaas stuck a notice up on the door post of the church saying that he, Kohlhaas, had set the city afire, and, if the Junker were not surrendered to him, he would raze the place so thoroughly that, as he put it, he would not have to hunt behind any walls to find him.

The terror of the Wittenbergians at this unheard-of outrage was indescribable; and no sooner had the fire, which luckily on that rather still summer night burned down no more than nineteen buildings (among them, however, one church) been partly extinguished toward morning, than the elderly Sheriff, Otto von Gorgas, dispatched a company of fifty men to capture the savage fellow. But the captain in command, whose name was Gerstenberg, managed things so badly that the whole expedition, instead of crushing Kohlhaas, only helped him to acquire a formidable military reputation: For when the captain split his force into squads so as to draw a ring around Kohlhaas and crush him, the latter, keeping his troop together, attacked his opponent at separate points and defeated him piecemeal, and by the evening of the following day not a man of the whole force on which the hopes of the country had been set stood against him in the field. Kohlhaas, who had lost a number of men in this encounter, again set fire to the city the next morning, his murderous efforts working so well this time that a great many houses and almost all the barns in Wittenberg's outskirts were burned to the ground. Posting his familiar manifesto again, indeed, on the corner walls of the City Hall itself, he appended to it an account of the utter defeat of Captain von Gerstenberg, whom the Sheriff had sent against him. The Sheriff was enraged by this display of defiance and placed himself with several knights at the head of a troop of one hundred and fifty men. At the Junker Wenzel von Tronka's written request, he gave the latter a guard to protect him against the violence of the people, who absolutely insisted on his being sent out of the city; and after he had posted sentinels in all the neighboring villages as well as on the city walls, to guard against a surprise attack, he sallied out himself on St. Jervis' Day to capture the dragon that was devastating the land. The horse dealer was sharp enough to give this force the slip; and after clever marching on his part, had drawn the Sheriff five leagues away from the city, where by various maneuvers Kohlhaas fooled him into thinking that he meant to withdraw into Brandenburg because of his opponent's superior force, he suddenly wheeled about at nightfall of the third day and made a forced march back to Wittenberg and set fire to the town a third time. Herse, who slipped into the city in disguise, was the one who carried out this terrible feat; and, because of the brisk north wind blowing, the fire spread so rapidly that in less than three hours' time forty-two houses, two churches, several convents and schools, and the Sheriff's own building were heaps of ashes. The Sheriff, who at daybreak believed that his adversary was in Brandenburg, marched back as fast as he could when he learned what had happened, to find the city in a general uproar; people by the thousands were besieging the Junker's house, which had been barricaded with heavy timbers and posts, and were shrieking at the top of their voices that he should be sent away. Two burgomasters named Jenkens and Otto, present in their official robes at the head of the assembled Town Council, tried in vain to persuade the crowd that they must wait for the return of a courier who had been dispatched to the President of the Chancery of State to seek permission for the Junker's removal to Dresden, where the knight himself had many reasons for wishing to go; but the unreasoning mob, armed with pikes and staves, paid no attention to their words and, after roughly handling some councilors who were demanding that vigorous measures should be taken, were on the point of storming the house and leveling it to the ground when the Sheriff, Otto von Gorgas, rode into the city at the head of his troop of horse. This worthy old knight, who was accustomed to inspiring the people to respectful obedience by his mere presence, had succeeded, by way of making up for the failure of the expedition from which he was returning, in taking prisoner, right in front of the city gates, three stray members of the incendiary's band; and while the fellows were put in chains before the eyes of the crowd, he made the Town Council a shrewd speech, assuring them that he was on Kohlhaas' track and that he thought he would soon be able to bring in the incendiary himself in chains: Thanks to all these reassurances, he was able to disarm the fears of the crowd and get them to accept the Junker's presence until the return of the courier from Dresden. He dismounted from his horse and, after having the posts and palisades cleared away, he entered the house, accompanied by some knights, where he found the Junker falling from one fainting fit into another while two attending physicians tried to bring him around with aromatics and stimulants; and since Sir Otto felt that this was no time to bandy words with him about the conduct he had been guilty of, he merely told the Junker, with a look of quiet contempt, that he should get dressed and follow him, for his own safety, to the knights' prison. When he appeared in the street wearing a doublet and a helmet they had put on him, with his chest half exposed on account of the difficulty he had in breathing, leaning on the arm of the Sheriff and his brother-in-law the Count von Gerschau, a shower of terrible curses fell on him. The people, whom the lansquenets had great difficulty in restraining, called him a bloodsucker, a miserable public pest, and a tormentor of men, the curse of Wittenberg and the ruin of Saxony; and, after a sorry march through the devastated streets, during which the Junker's helmet fell off several times without his missing it and was clapped back on his head by the knight walking behind him, they reached the prison at last; protected by a strong guard, he disappeared into a tower dungeon. Meanwhile the return of the courier with the Elector's resolution aroused fresh alarm in the city. For the Saxon government, to whom the citizens of Dresden had appealed directly in an urgent petition, refused to hear of the Junker's staying in the capital before the incendiary had been captured; instead, it called on the Sheriff, with all the forces at his command, to protect the Junker where he was, since he had to be somewhere; at the same time, so as to quiet their fears, it told the good city of Wittenberg that a force of five hundred men under Prince Friedrich of Meissen was already on its way to guard them from any further molestation by Kohlhaas. The Sheriff saw clearly that such a decree would never pacify the people: For not only had several small victories, which the horse dealer won outside the city, given rise to extremely disquieting rumors about the size his band had grown to, but his way of waging war in the black of night, with ruffians in disguise and with pitch, straw, and sulphur, unheard of and quite unprecedented as it was, would have baffled an even larger force than the one advancing under the Prince of Meissen. After a moment's reflection, Sir Otto decided to suppress completely the decree he had received. He merely posted a letter from the Prince of Meissen at all the street corners, announcing the latter's coming; at daybreak a covered wagon rumbled out of the courtyard of the knights' prison and took the road to Leipzig, accompanied by four heavily armed troopers who let it be known, though not in so many words, that they were bound for the Pleissenburg; and the people having thus been satisfied concerning the disaster-breeding Junker, whose whole existence seemed involved with fire and sword, the Sheriff set out with three hundred men to join forces with the Prince of Meissen.

Meanwhile Kohlhaas' force, thanks to the strange position the horse dealer had won for himself in the world, had grown to one hundred and nine men; and since he had also managed to lay hands on a store of weapons in Jessen, with which he armed his band to the teeth, he decided, on learning about the two armies bearing down on him, to march against them with the speed of the wind before they could join forces to overwhelm him. Accordingly he attacked the Prince of Meissen the very next night, surprising him near Mühlberg; however, in this battle, to his great grief, he lost Herse, who was struck down at his side by the first volley; but, furious at this loss, he gave such a drubbing to the Prince, who was unable to form his men up in the town, that the several severe wounds the latter got in the three hours' battle and the utter disorder into which his troops were thrown forced him to retreat to Dresden. Foolhardy from his victory, Kohlhaas turned back to attack the Sheriff before he learned about it, fell upon him at midday in the open country near the village of Damerow, and fought him till nightfall, suffering murderous losses, to be sure, but winning corresponding success. The next morning he would certainly have renewed the battle with the remnant of his band if the Sheriff, who had taken up a position in the Damerow churchyard, had not learned the news of the Prince's defeat at Mühlberg from scouts and therefore deemed it wiser to retreat, too, to Wittenberg, to await a more favorable opportunity. Five days after routing these two forces, Kohlhaas stood before the gates of Leipzig and set fire to the city on three sides.

In the manifesto which he scattered abroad on this occasion, he called himself "a viceroy of the Archangel Michael, come to punish with fire and sword, for the wickedness into which the whole world was sunk, all those who should take the side of the Junker in this quarrel." And from the castle at Lützen, which he had taken by surprise and in which he had established himself, he summoned the people to join with him to build a better order of things. With a kind of madness, the manifesto was signed: "Done at the Seat of Our Provisional World Government, the Chief Castle at Lützen." It was the good luck of the Leipzigers that a steady rain falling from the skies kept the fire from spreading, and, thanks to the speedy work of the fire stations, only a few small shops around the Pleissenburg went up in flames. Nevertheless, the presence of the desperate incendiary, with his delusion that the Junker was in Leipzig, gave rise to unspeakable dismay in the city, and when a troop of one hundred and eighty horse that had been sent against him came fleeing back in rout, nothing remained for the City Council, which did not wish to jeopardize the wealth of Leipzig, but to bar the gates completely and set the citizens to standing watch day and night outside the walls. It was useless for the Council to post notices in the villages roundabout swearing the Junker was not in the Pleissenburg; the horse dealer posted his own notices insisting that he was, and if he was not in the Pleissenburg he, Kohlhaas, would anyhow act as if he were until he was told where he was. The Elector, notified by courier of Leipzig's peril, announced that he was assembling a force of two thousand men, which he would lead himself to capture Kohlhaas. He sternly rebuked Otto von Gorgas for the ambiguous and thoughtless stratagem he had used to divert the incendiary from the neighborhood of Wittenberg. But it is impossible to describe the confusion that seized all Saxony, and especially its capital, when it was learned there that a notice addressed to Kohlhaas had been posted in all the villages around Leipzig, no one knew by whom, saying: "Wenzel the Junker is with his cousins Hinz and Kunz in Dresden."

It was in these circumstances that Doctor Martin Luther, relying on the authority that his position in the world gave him, tried to get Kohlhaas, by persuasion, to return within the confines of the social order;

building upon an element of good in the incendiary's breast, he had a notice posted in all the cities and market towns of the Electorate which read as follows:

Kohlhaas, you who say you are sent to wield the sword of justice, what are you doing, presumptuous man, in the madness of your blind fury, you who are yourself filled with injustice from head to foot? Because the sovereign to whom you owe obedience had denied you your rights, rights in a quarrel over a miserable possession, you rise up, wretch, with fire and sword and, like a wolf of the desert, descend on the peaceful community he protects. You who lead men astray with this declaration full of untruthfulness and cunning: Sinner, do you think it will avail you anything before God on that day whose light shall beam into the recesses of every heart? How can you say your rights have been denied you, whose savage breast, lusting for a base private revenge, gave up all attempts to find justice after your first thoughtless efforts came to nothing? Is a bench of constables and beadles who suppress a petition that has been presented to them or withhold a judgment it is their duty to deliver—is this your supreme authority? And need I tell you, impious man, that your sovereign knows nothing about your case: What am I saying?—the sovereign you are rebelling against does not even know your name, so that one day when you come before the throne of God thinking to accuse him, he will be able to say with a serene face, 'I have done this man no wrong, Lord, for my soul is a stranger to his existence.' The sword you bear, I tell you, is the sword of brigandage and bloodthirstiness, you are a rebel and no soldier of the just God, and your goal on earth is the wheel and the gallows, and in the hereafter the doom that is decreed for crime and godlessness.

MARTIN LUTHER
Wittenberg, etc.

At the castle in Lützen, Kohlhaas was just turning over in his mind a new plan for burning Leipzig—for he gave no credence to the notices in the villages saying that the Junker was in Dresden, since they were not signed by anybody, let alone the City Council, as he had demanded—when Sternbald and Waldmann were unpleasantly surprised to notice Luther's placard, which had been posted on the castle gate during the night. For several days the two men hoped in vain that Kohlhaas would catch sight of it himself, since they did not want to have to tell him about it; but though he came out in the evening, it was only to give a few brief commands, he was too gloomy and preoccupied to notice anything, until finally on a morning when two of his men were to hang for violating orders and looting in the neighborhood, they decided to draw it to his attention. He was just returning from the place of execution, with the pomp that he had adopted since the proclamation of his latest manifesto—a large archangelic sword was borne before him on a red leather cushion ornamented with gold tassels, while twelve men with burning torches followed after—and the people were timidly making way for him on either side, when Sternbald and Waldmann, with their swords tucked under their arms, begun to march demonstratively around the pillar with the placard on it, in a way that could not fail to excite his wonder. With his hands clasped behind his back, lost in his own thoughts, Kohlhaas had reached the portal when he looked up and stopped short; perceiving the two men respectfully drawing back, he strode rapidly to the pillar with his eyes still fixed absentmindedly on them. But who can describe the turmoil in his soul when he saw there the paper that accused him of injustice: signed by the dearest and most revered name he knew, the name of Martin Luther! A dark flush spread across his face. Taking off his helmet, he read the notice twice over from beginning to end; turned back among his men with an uncertain look as if he were about to say something, yet said nothing; took down the sheet from the pillar; read it through again; cried, "Waldmann, saddle my horse!" then, "Sternbald, follow me into the castle!" and disappeared inside. It needed no more than these few words to disarm him instantly, amid all the death and destruction in which he stood. He disguised himself as a Thuringian farmer; told Stembald that very important business made it necessary for him to go to Wittenberg; turned over the command of the band in Lützen to him in the presence of the leading men; and, with a promise to be back within three days, during which time there was no fear of an attack, rode off.

In Wittenberg he put up at an inn under an assumed name, and at nightfall, wrapped in his cloak and armed with a brace of pistols picked up in the sack of Tronka Castle, he entered Luther's room. Luther, who was sitting at his desk surrounded by books and manuscripts, when he saw the stranger open the door and bolt it behind him, asked him who he was and what he wanted; and no sooner had the man, who held his hat respectfully in his hand, replied with diffident anticipation of the dread his name would arouse, that he was Michael Kohlhaas, the horse dealer, than Luther cried, "Get out of here!" and, rising from the desk and hurrying toward a bell, he added, "Your breath is pestilence, your presence ruination!" Without stirring from the spot, Kohlhaas drew his pistol and said, "Your Reverence, if you touch that bell this pistol will stretch me lifeless at your feet! Sit down and hear what I have to say; you are safer with me than you are among the angels whose psalms you are inscribing." Luther sat down and said, "What do you want?"

"To show you you are wrong to think I am an unjust man! In your notice you told me that my sovereign knows nothing about my case: Very well, get me a safe-conduct and I will go to Dresden and lay it before him."

"Impious and terrible man!" cried Luther, puzzled and at the same time reassured by these words. "Who gives you the right to attack the Junker von Tronka on the authority of your own decree and, when you cannot find him in his castle, to punish the entire community that shelters him with fire and sword?"

Kohlhaas replied, "Your Reverence, nobody from now on! A report I got from Dresden deceived me, misled me! The war I am waging against society is a crime only as long as I have not been cast out of it, as you now assure me I have not been."

"Cast out of society!" exclaimed Luther, staring at him. "What kind of crazy ideas have got hold of you? How could anyone cast you out of the community of the state in which you live? Where, indeed, as long as states have existed has there ever been a case of anybody, no matter who, being cast out of society?"

"I call that man an outcast," Kohlhaas said, clenching his fist, "who is denied the protection of the laws! For I need this protection if my peaceful calling is to prosper; yes, it is for the protection that its laws afford me and mine that I seek shelter in the community; and whoever denies me it thrusts me out among the beasts of the wilderness; he is the one—how can you deny it?—who puts into my hand the club that I defend myself with."

"Who has denied you the protection of the laws?" cried Luther. "Didn't I write you that the sovereign to whom you addressed your complaint knows nothing about it? If state servants behind his back suppress lawsuits or otherwise make a mockery of his sacred name without his knowledge, who else but God has the right to call him to account for choosing such servants? Do you think, accursed and dreadful man, that you are entitled to judge him for it?"

"Very well," Kohlhaas replied, "if the sovereign has not cast me out of the community under his protection, I will return to it. Get me, I repeat, a safe-conduct to Dresden and I will disperse the band I have collected in the castle at Lützen and again lay my rejected complaint before the courts of the land." Luther, looking annoyed, shuffled the papers that were lying on his desk and made no reply. He was irritated by the defiant attitude this singular man took toward the state; and after thinking about the sentence Kohlhaas had passed on the Junker from Kohlhaasenbrück, he asked him what he wanted from the Dresden court. Kohlhaas answered, "Punishment of the Junker according to the law; restoration of my horses to their previous condition; and compensation for the damages that I as well as my man Herse, who fell at Mühlberg, suffered from the violence done us."

"Compensation for damages!" Luther cried. "You have borrowed by the thousands, from Jews and Christians, on notes and securities, to meet the expenses of your private revenge. Shall all that be counted in the final reckoning, too?"

"God forbid!" said Kohlhaas. "I don't ask back my house and farm and wealth, any more than the cost of my wife's funeral! Herse's old mother will present a bill for her son's medical costs, as well as a list of those things which he lost at Tronka Castle; and the government can have an expert estimate the loss I suffered by not selling the black horses."

Luther said, "Mad, incomprehensible, and terrible fellow!" and looked at him. "Now that your sword has taken the most ferocious revenge imaginable upon the Junker, what makes you insist on a judgment which, if it is finally pronounced, will weigh so lightly on him?"

Kohlhaas answered, as a tear rolled down his cheek, "Your Reverence, that judgment has cost me my wife; Kohlhaas means to show the world that she perished in no unrighteous quarrel. You yield to me in this point and let the court pronounce its judgment, and I will yield to you in all the other disputed points that come up."

Luther said, "Look here, what you are asking is only right, unless the circumstances are different from what the common report says they are; and if you had only managed to have your suit decided by the sovereign before you took your revenge in your own hands, I don't doubt that every one of your demands would have been granted. But all things considered, wouldn't you have done better to have pardoned the Junker for your Redeemer's sake, taken back the pair of blacks thin and worn out as they were, and mounted and ridden to Kohlhaasenbrück to fatten them in your own stable?"

"Perhaps so," Kohlhaas said, walking over to the window, "perhaps not, either! If I had known that it would need my dear wife's blood to put the horses back on their feet again, I might perhaps have done as your Reverence says and not made a business of a bushel of oats. But since they have cost me so dear now, let the thing run its course, say I; let judgment be pronounced as is my due, and let the Junker fatten my pair of blacks."

Luther took up his papers again, amid all sorts of thoughts, and said he would negotiate for Kohlhaas with the Elector. Meanwhile he would like him to stay quietly in the castle at Lützen; if the sovereign consented to grant him safe-conduct, he would be informed of it by the posting of a public notice. "Of course," he continued, as Kohlhaas bent to kiss his hand, "I don't know whether the Elector will choose mercy over justice, for I understand that he has got an army together and means to capture you in the castle at Lützen; but meanwhile, as I have already told you, there shan't be any lack of effort on my part." And he got up from the chair to dismiss him. Kohlhaas said that the fact that he was interceding for him put his mind completely at rest on that score; whereupon Luther waved him goodbye, but Kohlhaas, abruptly falling on one knee before him, said he had still another favor to ask. The fact was that at Pentecost, when it was his custom to receive Holy Communion, he had failed to go to church because of the military operations he was engaged in; would Luther have the goodness to hear his confession, without further preparation, and grant him in exchange the blessing of the Holy Sacrament? Luther, after a moment's thought in which he looked sharply at him, said,

"All right, Kohlhaas, I'll do it. But the Lord Whose body you hunger to have forgave His enemy. Will you likewise," he said as the other looked at him in surprise, "forgive the Junker who has offended you? Will you go to Tronka Castle, mount your pair of blacks, and ride them back to Kohlhaasenbrück to fatten them there?"

"Your Reverence—" Kohlhaas said, flushing, and seized his hand.

"Well?"

"—even the Lord did not forgive all his enemies. I am ready to forgive my two lords the Electors, the castellan and the steward, the lords Hinz and Kunz, and whoever else has done me wrong in this affair: But, if at all possible, let me have the Junker fatten my two blacks for me."

At these words Luther turned his back on him with a displeased look and rang the bell. Kohlhaas, wiping his eyes, rose from his knees in confusion as a famulus entered the anteroom with a light, in response to the summons; and as the latter vainly rattled the bolted door, Luther meanwhile having sat down to his papers again, Kohlhaas drew the bolt and let the man in. Luther looked sideways for an instant at the stranger and said to the famulus, "Light him out," upon which the latter, surprised to see a visitor, took down the key to the house door from the wall and, returning to the half-opened door, waited for the stranger to leave. Kohlhaas, taking his hat nervously in both hands, said, "And so, your Reverence, I cannot have the comfort of the reconciliation I asked you for?"

Luther answered curtly, "With your Savior, no; with the sovereign—that depends on the effort I promised to make for you." And he motioned to his famulus to perform the service he had called him in for without further ado. Kohlhaas pressed both hands to his breast with an expression of painful emotion, followed the man who lighted him down the stair, and vanished.

The next morning Luther sent a message to the Elector of Saxony in which, after bitterly alluding to the lords Hinz and Kunz von Tronka, Chamberlain and Cupbearer to His Highness, who, as everybody knew, were the ones who had suppressed Kohlhaas' petition, he told him with characteristic candor that under these difficult circumstances there was nothing for it but to accept the horse dealer's proposal and grant him an amnesty so that he might be able to renew his suit. Public opinion, Luther remarked, was on his side to a very dangerous extent, so much so that even in Wittenberg, which had been set on fire three times by him, it was still possible to hear voices raised in his favor; and since Kohlhaas would undoubtedly let the people know about it if his proposal were refused, as well as make his own malicious commentary on the matter, the populace might easily be misled so far that the state would find itself powerless to act against him. He concluded that, in such an extraordinary case, any scruples about entering into negotiations with a subject who had taken up arms against the state must be set aside; that, as a matter of fact, the wrong done Kohlhaas had in a certain sense placed him outside the social union; and in short, so as to put an end to the matter, he should be regarded rather as a foreign power that had attacked the country (and since he was not a Saxon subject, he really might in a way be regarded as such) than as a rebel in revolt against the throne.

When the Elector received this letter, there were present in the palace Prince Christiern of Meissen, Commander-in-Chief of the Realm, uncle of the Prince Friedrich of Meissen who had been defeated at Mühlberg and was still laid up with his wounds; the Lord High Chancellor Count Wrede; Count Kallheim, President of the Chancery of State; and the two lords Hinz and Kunz von Tronka, Cupbearer and Chamberlain, both intimate friends of the sovereign from his youth. The Chamberlain, Sir Kunz, who in his capacity of privy councilor attended to the private correspondence of his master and was authorized to use his name and seal, was the first to speak, and after again explaining in detail that he would never on his own authority have suppressed the complaint that the horse dealer brought against his cousin the Junker if it had not been for the fact that he had been misled by false statements into thinking it an unfounded and idle piece of mischief-making, he went on to consider the present state of affairs. He observed that neither divine nor human laws justified the horse dealer in taking such terrible vengeance as he had allowed himself for this mistake; dwelt on the renown that would fall on his accursed head if they treated with him as with a recognized military power; and the ignominy thus reflected upon the sacred person of the Elector seemed so intolerable to him that, carried away by his own eloquence, he said he would rather see the worst happen, which was for the mad rebel's sentence to be carried out and his cousin the Junker marched off to Kohlhaasenbrück to fatten his horses, than for Dr. Luther's proposal to be accepted.

The Lord Chancellor, Count Wrede, half turning toward Sir Kunz, expressed regret that his conduct at the start of this unquestionably awkward business had not been inspired with the same tender solicitude for the reputation of the sovereign as he now displayed in his proposal to settle it. He explained to the Elector the hesitation he felt about using the power of the state to enforce a manifest injustice; remarked, with a significant allusion to the followers the horse dealer was continually recruiting in the country, that the thread of the crime threatened to be spun out indefinitely, and declared that the only way to sever it and extricate the government from an ugly situation was to deal honestly with the man and make good, directly and without respect of person, the mistake they had been guilty of.

Prince Christiem of Meissen, when asked by the Elector to give his opinion, turned deferentially to the Lord Chancellor and said that the latter's reasoning naturally inspired him with the greatest respect; but in wishing to help Kohlhaas get justice for himself, the Chancellor overlooked the injury he did to the claims of Wittenberg, Leipzig, and all the country that the horse dealer had scourged in attempting to enforce his own rightful claim to compensation or at least punishment. The order of the state, as regards this man, was so disturbed that it needed more than an axiom borrowed from the science of jurisprudence to set it right. Therefore he agreed with the Chamberlain in favoring the use of the means appointed for such cases: They should get together a force large enough to capture or crush the horse dealer at Lützen.

The Chamberlain, bringing over two chairs from the wall and deferentially setting them down in the room for the Elector and the Prince, said that he was delighted to find a man of such integrity and acumen agreeing with him about the way to settle this puzzling business. The Prince took hold of the chair without sitting down and, looking him right in the face, assured him he had little reason to rejoice, since the first step such a course of action required was to issue a warrant for his, Sir Kunz's, arrest, followed by his trial on charges of misusing the sovereign's name. For though it was necessary to veil from the eyes of justice a series of crimes that led endlessly on to further crimes, for all of which there was not room enough before the throne of judgment, this was not the case with the original offense from which everything had sprung; and the very first thing the state must do was to try the Chamberlain for his life, if it was to own the authority to crush the horse dealer, whose grievance, as they well knew, was exceedingly just and into whose hands they themselves had put the sword he now wielded.

The Elector, toward whom the discomfited Chamberlain looked at these words, turned away, his whole face reddening, and went to the window. Count Kallheim, after an embarrassed silence on everyone's part, said that this was not the way to extricate themselves from the magic circle in which they were caught. With equal justice they might put his nephew Prince Friedrich on trial; for in the strange expedition that he had led against Kohlhaas he had overstepped his instructions in all sorts of ways, and if one were to draw up the long list of those responsible for the embarrassment in which they now found themselves, his name too would figure in it and he would have to be called to account by the sovereign for the events at Mühlberg.

As the Elector, with a perplexed look, walked over to his desk, the Cupbearer, Sir Hinz von Tronka, began to speak in his turn: He could not understand how the right course for the state to follow in this matter had escaped men as wise as those assembled here. The horse dealer, as he understood it, had promised to disband his company in return for a simple safe-conduct to Dresden and the renewal of the inquiry into his case. But it did not follow from this that he must be granted an amnesty for criminally taking his revenge into his own hands: These were two entirely separate matters, which Dr. Luther as well as the Council of State seemed to have confounded. "After," he continued, laying his finger alongside of his nose, "the Dresden court has pronounced judgment, whatever it may be, in the matter of the black horses, nothing prevents us from arresting Kohlhaas for his incendiarism and brigandage: a politic solution that unites the advantages of both statesmen's views and is certain to win the approbation of the world and of posterity." As the only reply both the Prince and the Lord Chancellor gave to the Cupbearer Sir Hinz's speech was a contemptuous look, and the discussion seemed at an end, the Elector said he would weigh in his mind, between now and the next sitting of the Council, the different opinions he had received.

Apparently the preliminary step contemplated by the Prince had killed all desire in the Elector, who was highly sensitive wherever friendship was concerned, to go ahead with the campaign against Kohlhaas, for which all the preparations were made. At any rate he detained the Lord Chancellor Count Wrede, whose opinion seemed to him the likeliest one, and let the others go; and when the latter showed him letters indicating that the horse dealer's strength had actually grown to some four hundred men—indeed, considering the general discontent in the country owing to the highhanded actions of the Chamberlain, he might count on doubling or tripling that number in a short time—he decided without further ado to accept Dr. Luther's advice. The entire management of the Kohlhaas affair was therefore handed over to Count Wrede; and only a few days later a notice was posted, the gist of which we give as follows:

We, etc., etc., Elector of Saxony, in especially gracious consideration of the intercession made to us by Dr. Martin Luther, do grant to Michael Kohlhaas, horse dealer of Brandenburg, safe-conduct to Dresden for the purpose of a renewed inquiry into his case, on condition that within three days after sight of this he lay down the arms which he has taken up; but it is understood that in the event that his complaint concerning the black horses is rejected by the court at Dresden, which is hardly likely, he shall be prosecuted with all the severity of the law for seeking to take justice into his own hands; in the contrary event, however, tempering our justice with mercy, we will grant him and all his band full amnesty for the acts of violence committed by him in Saxony.

Kohlhaas had no sooner received from Dr. Luther a copy of this notice which had been posted in every public square in the land, than he went ahead, in spite of the conditions it made, and disbanded his following, whom he sent away with gifts, expressions of his gratitude, and suitable admonitions. Whatever he had captured in the way of money, weapons, and military stores he deposited with the courts at Lützen as the property of the Elector; and after sending Waldmann and Sternbald off, the one to the bailiff at Kohlhaasenbrück with letters proposing to repurchase his farm, if that were possible, and the other to Schwerin to fetch his children whom he wished to have by his side again, he left the castle at

Lützen and, carrying the remnant of his little property on his person in the form of notes, he made his way unrecognized to Dresden.

Day was just breaking and the whole city still lay asleep as he knocked at the door of the little dwelling in the suburb of Pirna which, thanks to the honesty of the bailiff, still belonged to him, and told his old servant Thomas, who looked after the place, when he opened the door and stared dumfounded at him, to go to the Government House and report to the Prince of Meissen that Kohlhaas the horse dealer had arrived. The Prince of Meissen, who thought it expedient to go at once and see how matters stood between them and this man, found an immense throng of people already gathered in the streets leading to Kohlhaas' house when he appeared soon after with a retinue of knights and men. The news of the presence of the avenging angel who chastised the oppressors of the people with fire and sword had aroused all of Dresden, city and suburbs; the door had to be bolted against the pressure of the curious crowd, and boys clambered up to the windows to catch a glimpse of the incendiary at his breakfast.

As soon as the Prince had made his way into the house with the help of a bodyguard that cleared a path for him and had entered Kohlhaas' room, he asked the horse dealer, whom he found standing half undressed at a table, whether he was Kohlhaas the horse dealer; whereupon the latter drew from his belt a wallet with papers in it dealing with his affairs, and, respectfully handing it to the Prince, he said yes, adding that after disbanding his company he had come to Dresden, under protection of the safe-conduct granted him by the sovereign, to press his suit against the Junker Wenzel von Tronka before the court. With a rapid glance the Prince took Kohlhaas in from head to foot, then looked through the papers in the wallet; had him explain the meaning of a certificate from the court at Lützen acknowledging a deposit in favor of the Electoral treasury; and, after asking him all sorts of questions about his children, his means, and the kind of life he intended to lead in the future, so as to see the kind of man he was, and concluding that they might set their minds at rest about him in all respects, gave him back his papers and said that nothing now stood in the way of his suit, and that all he need do to commence proceedings was to apply directly himself to the Lord High Chancellor of the Tribunal, Count Wrede. "In the meantime," said the Prince after a pause, as he crossed over to the window and looked out in astonishment at the crowd in front of the house, "you must have a guard for the first few days to protect you in your house and when you go out."

Kohlhaas looked down, disconcerted, and said nothing.

"Well then, never mind," said the Prince, coming away from the window. "If anything happens, you have only yourself to blame for it," and he turned to the door to leave. Kohlhaas, who had had some second thoughts, said, "My Lord, do as you like! If you give me your word the guard will be withdrawn whenever

I wish it, I have no objection." The Prince replied that that was understood; and after telling the three lansquenets detailed for the duty that the man whose house they were staying in was completely at liberty and that it was merely for his own protection that they were to follow him when he went out, he saluted the horse dealer with an easy wave of the hand and left.

Toward midday, escorted by his three lansquenets and trailed by an immense crowd whom the police had warned against offering him any harm, Kohlhaas went to visit the Lord Chancellor, Count Wrede. The Chancellor received him with great kindness in his ante-chamber and, after talking with him two whole hours and hearing Kohlhaas' story from beginning to end, he referred him to a celebrated lawyer in the city, one who was a colleague of the court, so that he might have the complaint drawn up and immediately presented. Kohlhaas did not lose a minute in going to the lawyer's house; and after having the suit drawn up exactly like the one which had been quashed—he asked for punishment of the Junker according to the law, restoration of the horses to their previous condition, and compensation for his damages and also for those suffered by his man Herse, who had fallen at Mühlberg, the latter to be paid to the groom's old mother—he returned home, still followed by the gaping crowd, his mind made up never to quit the house again unless his affairs absolutely required it.

Meanwhile, the Junker had been released from his prison in Wittenberg and, after getting over a dangerous attack of erysipelas that had inflamed his foot, he had been peremptorily summoned to appear before the Dresden court to answer the charges made against him by the horse dealer Kohlhaas concerning a pair of black horses that had been unlawfully taken from him and ruined by overwork. The two brothers von Tronka, cousins of the Junker, at whose house he came to stay, received him with the greatest bitterness and contempt; they called him a worthless wretch who had brought shame and disgrace on the whole family, told him he was sure to lose his suit, and to get ready to produce the pair of blacks which he would be condemned to fatten to the accompaniment of the scornful laughter of the world. The Junker answered in a weak and quavering voice that he was the most pitiable man alive. He swore he had known very little about the whole damned business that had brought him so much misfortune, and that the castellan and the steward were to blame for everything, for they had used the horses to get the harvest in without his remotest knowledge or consent and worked them until they were skin and bones, part of the time too in their own fields. Sitting down as he said this, he begged them not to abuse and insult him and bring back the illness from which he had only recently recovered. The next day the lords Hinz and Kunz, who owned property in the vicinity of the ruins of Tronka Castle, wrote, at the urging of their cousin the Junker, since there was nothing else to do, to ask their steward and tenants for information about the two black horses that had disappeared on that unhappy day without being heard of since. But because the castle had been completely destroyed and most of its inhabitants massacred, all they could discover was that a stable boy, beaten with the flat of the incendiary's sword, had rescued them from the burning shed, and that afterwards, when the boy had asked him where to take the horses and what to do with them, the crazy fellow had answered him with a kick. The Junker's gouty old housekeeper, who had fled to Meissen, assured him, in reply to his written inquiry, that on the morning after that terrible night the stable boy had gone off with the horses toward the Brandenburg border; but all the inquiries made there proved vain, and anyhow there seemed to be an error at the bottom of this information, since none of the Junker's people came from Brandenburg or even from somewhere along the road to it. Some men from Dresden who had been in Wilsdruf a few days after the burning of Tronka Castle said that a groom had turned up there about that time leading two horses by the halter, and, since the animals were on their last legs and could not go any further, he had left them with a shepherd who had offered to feed them back to health in his barn. For a variety of reasons, it seemed quite probable that these were the pair of blacks in question; but the shepherd of Wilsdruf, according to the people had just come from there, had already disposed of them again, no one knew to whom; and a third rumor, whose author could not be discovered, had the two horses quite simply dead and buried in the Wilsdruf boneyard.

The lords Hinz and Kunz found this turn of affairs extremely welcome, as can readily be imagined, for it spared them the necessity (since their cousin the Junker no longer had any stables of his own) of fattening the horses in theirs, but they wanted to verify the story so as to be absolutely sure. Consequently Junker Wenzel von Tronka, as lord of the demesne, liege lord, and lord justice, addressed a letter to the magistrates at Wilsdruf minutely describing the horses, which he said had been placed in his care and accidentally lost, and requesting them to be so good as to ascertain their present whereabouts and to urge and admonish their owner, whoever he might be, to deliver them to the stables of the Chamberlain Sir Kunz in Dresden, where he would be generously reimbursed for all his costs. And a few days later the man to whom the shepherd at Wilsdruf had sold the horses did in fact appear with them, cadaverous creatures stumbling at the tail of his cart, and led them to the Dresden market place; but as the bad luck of Sir Wenzel and still more of honest Kohlhaas would have it, he turned out to be the knacker of Döbbeln.

As soon as the rumor reached Sir Wenzel, in the presence of his cousin the Chamberlain, that a man had arrived in the city with the two black horses that had escaped from the Tronka Castle fire, the two of them, after hurriedly rounding up some servants from the house, went down to the palace square where the fellow was, intending, if the animals proved to be Kohlhaas', to pay him the money he had spent on them and take the horses home with them. But the knights were surprised to see a crowd, whom the spectacle had attracted, already gathered around the two-wheeled cart to which the horses were tied and getting bigger by the minute; laughing uproariously, the people shouted to one another that the horses on whose account the foundations of the state were tottering were already in the knacker's hands! The Junker, after walking around the cart and staring at the miserable creatures who looked as if they were going to die any minute, mumbled in embarrassment: They were not the horses he had taken from Kohlhaas; but Sir Kunz the Chamberlain, throwing him a look of speechless rage, which if it had been made of iron would have smashed him to bits, and flinging back his cloak to show his orders and his chain of office, strode over to the knacker and said: Were those the black horses that the shepherd of Wilsdruf had got hold of and that the Junker Wenzel von Tronka, to whom they belonged, had commandeered from the magistrate of that place? The knacker, who had a pail of water in his hand and was giving a drink to the fat and sturdy nag that drew his cart, said, "The blacks?" Then, putting down the pail and slipping the bit out of the horse's mouth, he said that the pair of blacks tied to the back of the cart had been sold to him by the swineherd of Hainichen. Where the latter had got them, and whether they came from the shepherd at Wilsdruf, he didn't know. He had been told, he said, taking up the pail again and propping it between the cart shaft and his knee—he had been told by the messenger from the Wilsdruf court to take the horses to the Tronka residence in Dresden; but the Junker he had been told to go to was named Kunz. And, turning away, he emptied the water his animal had left in the pail onto the pavement. The Chamberlain found it impossible to get the fellow, who went about his business with phlegmatic diligence, to look at him, and said, amid the stares of the jeering crowd, that he was the Chamberlain Kunz von Tronka; the pair of blacks he was looking for were the ones belonging to his cousin, the Junker; they had been given to the shepherd at Wilsdruf by a groom who ran away from Tronka Castle at the time it was sacked, and originally they had belonged to the horse dealer Kohlhaas. He asked the fellow, who stood there with his legs astraddle, hitching up his pants, whether he didn't know something about all this. Hadn't the swineherd from Hainichen perhaps bought the horses from the Wilsdruf shepherd—for everything depended on that—or from a third person who had got them from the shepherd?

The knacker, after standing up against the cart and passing water, said he had been told to go to Dresden with the horses where he could get the money for them at the Tronka house. He didn't understand what the Chamberlain was talking about; whether Peter or Paul or the shepherd of Wilsdruf had owned them before the swineherd in Hainichen was all one to him so long as they hadn't been stolen.

And, cocking his whip across his broad back, he shambled off toward a public house that stood in the square, with the intention, since he was hungry, of getting himself some breakfast. The Chamberlain, who did not for the life of him know what to do with the horses the swineherd of Hainichen had sold to the knacker of Döbbeln, unless they were the ones the devil himself was galloping around Saxony on, asked the Junker to say something; but when the latter replied, with white and quivering lips, that the best thing to do under the circumstances was to buy the blacks whether they were Kohlhaas' or not, the Chamberlain flung his cloak back and, cursing the father and mother who had made him, strode out of the crowd, absolutely at a loss to know what he should do. He called over Baron von Wenk, a friend of his who happened to be riding along the street, and asked him to stop by at the house of the Lord Chancellor Count Wrede and have the latter arrange for Kohlhaas to come out to examine the pair of blacks; for he was stubbornly determined not to quit the square just because the mob were looking at him mockingly, their handkerchiefs crammed into their mouths, and only waiting for him to leave, it seemed, to burst out laughing. Now it so happened that Kohlhaas was at the Lord Chancellor's, where he had been summoned by a court messenger to explain some matters in connection with the deposit he had made in Lützen, when the Baron entered the room on his errand; and when the Chancellor got up from his chair with a look of annoyance, leaving the horse dealer standing with his papers to one side, the Baron, who did not know Kohlhaas, explained the difficulty in which the lords von Tronka found themselves. The knacker from Döbbeln, he said, acting on a defective requisition of the Wilsdruf court, had turned up with a pair of horses in such hopeless condition that it was no wonder the Junker Wenzel hesitated to recognize them as Kohlhaas'; but if they were going to be accepted from the knacker notwithstanding and an attempt made to put them in shape again in the knights' stables, an ocular inspection by Kohlhaas was needed so as to remove all doubt. "Will you therefore be good enough," he concluded, "to have a guard fetch the horse dealer from his house and conduct him to the market place where the horses are?" The Lord Chancellor took his glasses from his nose and said to the Baron that he was laboring under a double misapprehension: first, in thinking that the question of the horses' ownership could only be decided by an ocular inspection by Kohlhaas; and then in imagining that he, the Chancellor, possessed the authority to have Kohlhaas taken by a guard to wherever the Junker happened to wish. Whereupon he introduced him to the horse dealer standing behind him and asked him, as he sat down and put his glasses back on, to apply to the man himself in the matter.

Kohlhaas, whose expression gave no hint of what was passing in his mind, said that he was ready to follow the Baron to the market place to inspect the knacker's horses. As the latter faced around to him in surprise,

Kohlhaas went up to the Chancellor's table again, gave him, with the help of the papers in his wallet, the information he needed about the deposit in Lützen, and said goodbye; the Baron, who with a crimson face had walked over to the window, likewise took his leave; and the two men, escorted by the Prince of Meissen's three lansquenets, made their way, with a crowd of people at their heels, to the palace square. The Chamberlain Sir Kunz, who meanwhile, over the protests of several friends who had joined him, had been standing his ground among the people opposite the knacker of Döbbeln, accosted the horse dealer as soon as he appeared with the Baron and asked him, as he tucked his sword with haughty ostentation under his arm, whether the horses standing at the cart tail were his. The horse dealer, after turning diffidently toward the unknown gentleman who had asked the question and touching his hat, moved over without answering to the knacker's cart, followed by all the knights; and, stopping twelve paces off from where the animals stood on unsteady legs with their heads bowed to the ground, refusing the hay the knacker had pitched out for them, he gave them one look, turned back to the Chamberlain, and said, "My lord, the knacker is quite right: The horses tied to his cart are mine." And then, looking around the circle of knights, he touched his hat again and left the square with his guard.

As soon as he heard this, the Chamberlain went across to the knacker at a jump that set his helmet plume nodding and tossed him a bag of money;

and while the latter scraped the hair back from his forehead with a lead comb and stared at the money in his hand, Sir Kunz ordered a servant to untie the horses and lead them home. The man left a group of his family and friends in the crowd at his master's summons and did, in fact, with a red face, step over a large pile of dung at the horses' feet and go up to their heads; but he had hardly taken hold of the halter to untie them when Master Himboldt, his cousin, grabbed him by the arm, and crying: "Don't you touch those knacker's nags!" pulled him away from the cart. Then stepping precariously back over the dung pile, the Master turned to the Chamberlain, who stood there speechless with surprise, and said: He must get a knacker's man to do him a service like that! The Chamberlain, livid with rage, looked at the Master for a second and then turned and shouted over the heads of the knights for the guard; and when, at Baron von Wenk's command, an officer emerged from the castle at the head of some of the Elector's gentlemen-at-arms, he gave him a brief account of the shameful way in which the burghers of the city were inciting to rebellion and called on him to arrest the ringleader, Master Himboldt. Catching the Master by his shirt, he accused him of mistreating the servant he had ordered to untie the black horses and pushing him away from the cart. The Master twisted skillfully out of the Chancellor's grasp and said, "My lord, showing a boy of twenty what he ought to do is not inciting to revolt! Ask him if he wants to go against everything that's customary and decent and meddle with those horses tied to the cart. If after what I've said his answer is yes, it's all right with me, he can start skinning them right now for all I care!"

The Chamberlain turned to the groom and asked him if he had any objection to carrying out his order to untie Kohlhaas' horses and lead them home; when the fellow, retreating into the crowd, timidly replied: The horses must be made decent and respectable again before that could be expected of him, the Chamberlain came right after him, knocked off his hat in which he wore the badge of the Tronka house, trampled it under his feet, and, drawing his sword, drove him from the square and out of his service. Master Himboldt cried, "Down with the murderous tyrant!" And while his fellow citizens, outraged by this scene, pressed shoulder to shoulder and forced back the guard, he knocked the Chamberlain down from behind, ripped his cloak, collar, and helmet off, wrenched the sword from his hand, and with a violent motion sent it clattering across the square. The Junker Wenzel, escaping from the tumult, called to the knights to go to his cousin's aid, but to no avail: Before they were able to take a step toward him, they were scattered by the rush of the mob, and the Chamberlain, who had hurt his head in falling, was exposed to their full fury. The only thing that saved him was the appearance of a troop of mounted lansquenets who happened to be crossing the square and whom the officer commanding the Elector's men called over to help him. The officer, after dispersing the crowd, seized the enraged Master and had some troopers lead him off to prison, while two of the Chamberlain's friends lifted the latter's blood-spattered form from the ground and carried him home. Such was the unhappy conclusion of the well-meant and honest attempt to procure the horse dealer satisfaction for the injustice done him. The Döbbeln knacker, as his business was done and he wished to be off, tied the horses to a lamp post when the crowd began to disperse and there they stayed the whole day through, without anybody's bothering about them, objects of ridicule for the ragamuffins and the idlers; but finally the police took charge of them for lack of anybody else, and toward evening they got the knacker of Dresden to carry them off to his yard outside the city until their disposition was decided.

The riot in the palace square, as little as Kohlhaas was to blame for it, nevertheless aroused a feeling throughout the land, even among the more moderate and better class of people, that was highly dangerous to the success of his suit. It was felt the state had got itself into an intolerable position vis-à-vis the horse dealer, and in private houses and public places alike the opinion grew that it would be better to do the man an open wrong and quash the whole proceedings again, than to see that justice, extorted by violence, was done him in so trivial a matter, just to satisfy his crazy obstinacy. To complete poor Kohlhaas' ruin, it was the Lord Chancellor himself, with his rigid honesty and his hatred of the Tronka family which sprang from it, who helped strengthen and spread this sentiment. It was most unlikely that the horses now in the hands of the Dresden knacker would ever be restored to the shape they were in when they left the stables at Kohlhaasenbrück, but even if this were possible through skillful, unremitting care, the disgrace that had fallen on the Junker's family as a result of everything that had happened was so great that nothing seemed fairer and more reasonable to people—seeing the important place the von Tronkas occupied in the government as one of the oldest and noblest houses in the country—than that they should pay Kohlhaas a money amends for the horses. Yet a few days later, when the President, Count Kallheim, acting for the Chamberlain who was laid up with his injuries, sent a letter to the Chancellor making just such a proposal, and even though the Chancellor wrote to Kohlhaas warning him against declining such an offer if one were made to him, he himself wrote the President a curt, barely civil reply asking to be excused from any private commissions in the matter, and advising the Chamberlain to address himself directly to the horse dealer, whom he described as a very reasonable and modest man. The horse dealer, whose iron determination had in fact been weakened by the incident in the market place, was ready, following the advice of the Chancellor, to meet any overture from the Junker or his kinsmen half way, with perfect willingness and forgiveness for everything that had happened; but just such an overture was more than the proud knights could stomach; and highly indignant at the answer they had received from the

Lord Chancellor, they showed it to the Elector the next morning when he came to visit the Chamberlain in the room where he was laid up with his wounds. The Chamberlain, in a voice that illness made weak and pathetic, asked the Elector whether, after risking his life to settle the business according to his sovereign's wishes, he must also expose his honor to the censure of the world by going hat in hand to beg indulgence from a man who had already heaped every imaginable shame and disgrace on him and his family. The Elector, after reading the letter, asked Count Kallheim in embarrassment if the court did not have the right, without consulting further with Kohlhaas, to take its stand on the fact that the horses were past recovery and bring in a verdict for a money amends, just as if the horses were already dead.

"Your Highness," the Count replied, "the horses *are* dead, legally dead because they have no value any more, and they will be physically dead before any one can get them from the knacker's yard to the knights' stables"; upon which the Elector tucked the letter in his pocket, said that he would speak to the Lord Chancellor about it himself, spoke reassuringly to the Chamberlain who had raised himself on his elbow and seized his hand in gratitude, and, after recommending him to watch his health, he rose with a benign air from his chair and left the room.

So matters stood in Dresden when poor Kohlhaas found himself the center of another, even more serious storm that came up from the direction of Lützen,

and whose lightning the crafty knights were clever
enough to draw down on his unlucky head. A man
called Johann Nagelschmidt, one of the band whom
the horse dealer had collected and then turned off
again after the Electoral amnesty, had some weeks
later rounded up a part of this rabble, which shrank
from nothing, on the Bohemian border, with the
intention of carrying on for himself the trade Kohlhaas
had taught him. This ruffian announced, partly to
scare the sheriff's officers on his heels, and partly to
get the peasantry to take a hand in his rascalities as
they had done with Kohlhaas, that he was Kohlhaas'
lieutenant; had it spread about, with a cleverness
learned from his master, that the amnesty had been
broken in the case of several men who had gone quietly back to their homes; that Kohlhaas himself,
indeed, with a perfidiousness that cried aloud to heav-
en, had been arrested on his arrival in Dresden and
placed under guard; the result of this being that the
incendiary crew were able to masquerade, in manifestoes very much like Kohlhaas' that Nagelschmidt
had posted up, as honest soldiers assembled together
for the sole purpose of serving God and watching over
the Elector's amnesty—all this, as has just been said,
done not at all for the glory of God nor out of attachment to Kohlhaas, whose fate the outlaws did not care
a straw about, but to enable them to burn and plunder
with the greater impunity and ease. When the first
word of this reached Dresden, the knights could not
conceal the joy they felt over a development that

seemed to put such a different face on things. With sage displeasure they recalled what a mistake it had been, in spite of their earnest and repeated warnings, to grant Kohlhaas an amnesty, going on as if there had been a deliberate intention to give every scoundrel in the country the signal to follow in the horse dealer's footsteps; and not content with accepting Nagelschmidt's claim that he had taken up arms only to defend his oppressed master, they expressed the certain opinion that his appearance on the scene was nothing but a plot on Kohlhaas' part to scare the government and hasten and assure a verdict that would satisfy his mad obstinacy down to the last detail. Indeed the Cupbearer, Sir Hinz, went so far as to say to some courtiers and hunting companions who had gathered around him after dinner in the Elector's antechamber that the disbanding of the brigands in Lützen had been nothing but a damned trick; and, while making fun of the Lord Chancellor's love of justice, he cleverly concatenated various facts to prove that the band was still intact in the forests of the Electorate and only waited for a signal from the horse dealer to burst forth afresh with fire and sword.

Prince Christiern of Meissen, who was highly displeased with this new turn of affairs, which threatened so much damage to his sovereign's reputation, went at once to the palace to see the Elector; and, clearly perceiving how the knights would wish to encompass Kohlhaas' ruin by convicting him of new offenses, he asked permission to question the horse dealer without delay. The horse dealer, not a little surprised at the summons, appeared at the Government House under a constable's escort with his two little boys, Heinrich and Leopold, in his arms for his five children had arrived the day before with Stembald from Mecklenburg where they had been staying, and for reasons too numerous to detail here Kohlhaas, when the two burst into childish tears on his getting up to leave and begged to be taken along, had picked them up and carried them to the hearing. The Prince, after looking benevolently at the children whom their father had seated beside him and asking them their names and ages with friendly interest, told Kohlhaas about the liberties that his old follower Nagelschmidt was taking in the valleys of the Erzgebirge; and, handing him the latter's so-called manifestoes, he asked him what he had to say in his own defense. The horse dealer, though indeed he showed extreme dismay when confronted with these treasonable documents, had little difficulty in satisfying a man as upright as the Prince that the accusations leveled against him were baseless. He not only did not see how he needed the help of a third person, as matters stood now, to obtain a judgment in his suit, which was progressing entirely satisfactorily, but he had papers with him which he showed to the Prince that made it appear most unlikely that Nagelschmidt should ever wish to give him such help: For shortly before the disbanding of his band at Lützen he had been on the point of hanging the fellow, for a rape committed in open country and other outrages, when the publication of the Electoral amnesty severed their connection and saved Nagelschmidt's life; the next day they had parted deadly enemies.

With the Prince's approval, Kohlhaas sat down and wrote a letter to Nagelschmidt, in which he called the latter's claim to having taken up arms to enforce the amnesty a shameless and wicked fabrication; on his arrival in Dresden, he told him, he had neither been jailed nor put under guard, also his lawsuit was progressing just as he wished; and he gave him over, because of the acts of arson Nagelschmidt had committed in the Erzgebirge after publication of the amnesty, to the full vengeance of the law, as a warning to the rabble around him. Extracts from Kohlhaas' trial of Nagelschmidt in the castle at Lützen on account of the above-mentioned crimes were appended to the letter, to inform the people about this scoundrel who already at that time was destined for the gallows and owed his life, as we have mentioned, only to the Elector's edict. Upon which the Prince soothed Kohlhaas' resentment over the suspicions that had unavoidably to be expressed at the hearing; promised him that as long as he remained in Dresden the amnesty would not be violated in any way; shook the boys' hands again as he made them a present of some fruit on the table; and said goodbye to Kohlhaas. Nevertheless, the Lord Chancellor recognized the danger hanging over the horse dealer's head and did everything in his power to press the lawsuit to a conclusion before new circumstances arose to complicate and confuse it; but to complicate and confuse the case was exactly what the crafty knights desired and intended. They no longer silently acknowledged the Junker's guilt and limited their efforts to obtaining a milder sentence for their cousin, but instead began to raise all sorts of cunning arguments and quibbling objections, so as to deny his guilt entirely. Sometimes they would pretend that Kohlhaas' horses had been detained at Tronka Castle by the castellan's and the steward's arbitrary action, and that the Junker had known little if anything about it; at other times they claimed the animals had been sick with a violent and dangerous cough when they arrived at the castle, and promised to produce witnesses to confirm the truth of what they said; and when, after lengthy investigations and explanations, they were forced to abandon these arguments, they fell back on an Electoral edict of twelve years' standing that in fact forbade importing horse stock from Brandenburg to Saxony on account of a cattle disease: clear proof that the Junker had not only the right but even the duty to seize the horses Kohlhaas had brought across the border.

Meanwhile Kohlhaas, who had repurchased his farm at Kohlhaassenbrück from the honest bailiff, paying him a small additional sum to reimburse him for the loss he suffered thereby, wished to leave Dresden for a few days and pay a visit to his home, apparently in order to settle the matter legally—in which decision, however, the above-mentioned consideration, pressing as it may actually have been on account of the need to sow the winter crop, undoubtedly played less part than a wish to test his position in the strange and dubious circumstances prevailing; and he may also have been influenced by still other reasons that we shall leave to those who know their own hearts to divine. Accordingly, leaving his guard at home, he went to the Lord Chancellor and, with the bailiff's letters in his hand, explained that if he was not needed in court now, as seemed to be the case, he would like to leave the city and travel to Brandenburg for some eight to twelve days, within which period he promised to return. The Lord Chancellor, looking down with an annoyed and doubtful face, expressed the opinion that Kohlhaas' presence was more necessary than ever just then, as the court required statements and explanations from him on a thousand and one points that might come up, to counter the cunning shifts and dodges of his opponent; but when Kohlhaas referred him to his lawyer, who was thoroughly posted on the case, and pressed his request with modest persistence, promising to limit his absence to a week, the Lord Chancellor, after a pause, only said, as he dismissed him, that he hoped he would apply to Prince Christiern of Meissen for a pass.

Kohlhaas, who could read the Lord Chancellor's face very well, was only strengthened in his determination and, sitting down on the spot and giving no reason, he asked the Prince of Meissen, as Chief of the Government, for a week's pass to Kohlhaasenbrück and back. In reply, he received an order from the Governor of the Palace, Baron Siegfried von Wenk, to the effect that his request to visit Kohlhaasenbrück would be laid before his Serene Highness the Elector, and as soon as the latter's consent was forthcoming the pass would be sent to him. When Kohlhaas asked his lawyer how the order came to be signed by a Baron Siegfried von Wenk and not by Prince Christiem of Meissen, to whom he had addressed his request, he was told that the Prince had left for his estates three days ago and that during his absence the affairs of his office had been turned over to the Governor of the Palace, Baron Siegfried von Wenk, a cousin of the gentleman of the same name whom we have already encountered.

Kohlhaas, whose heart began to pound uneasily amid all these complications, waited several more days for an answer to his request, which had been submitted to the sovereign with such surprising formality; but when a week and more had passed without his either receiving a reply or the court's handing down a judgment in his case even though it had been promised him without fail, he sat down on the twelfth day, his mind made up to force the Government to reveal its intentions toward him, whatever they might be, and earnestly petitioned the Government once again for a pass. But on the evening of the following day, which had likewise passed without his getting the answer he was expecting, going over to the window of his little back room with his mind very much on his present situation and especially the amnesty Dr. Luther had got for him, he was thunderstruck to see no sign, in the little outbuilding in the yard which was their quarters, of the guard assigned him on his arrival by the Prince of Meissen. Thomas, his old servant, whom he called to him and asked the meaning of this, said with a sigh: "Sir, there's something wrong; there were more lansquenets here today than usual and at nightfall they posted themselves around the whole house: Two of them, with their shields and pikes, are standing out in the street in front of the house door; two more are at the back door in the garden; and still another pair are stretched out on some straw in the entrance hall where they say they are going to spend the night."

Kohlhaas' face paled; turning away, he said it didn't really matter, seeing that they were there already; when Thomas went down to the hall, he should put a light there so they could see. And, after he had opened the front shutters on the pretext of emptying a pot and convinced himself of the truth of Thomas' words, for just at that moment he saw the guard silently being changed—something no one had ever thought of doing since the arrangement existed—he went to bed, even though he did not feel much like sleeping, with his mind instantly made up about what he would do the next day. For what he disliked most about the regime he had to deal with was the show of justice it put on, at the same time that it went ahead and broke the amnesty which he had been promised; if he was in fact a prisoner, as he could no longer doubt, he was going to make them say so straight out. Accordingly, the next morning he had Stembald hitch up his wagon and bring it around to the door; he meant, he said, to drive to Lockewitz to see the steward there, an old friend of his who had spoken to him a few days before in Dresden and invited him to pay him a visit with his children. The lansquenets, having watched with huddled heads the stir these preparations made in the household, secretly sent one of their number into town, and a few minutes later an official of the Government marched up at the head of some constables and went into the house across the way as if he had business there. Kohlhaas was busy getting his children's clothes on, but he did not miss these goings-on and purposely kept the wagon waiting in front of the house longer than was really necessary; as soon as he saw the police had taken up their posts, he came out in front of the house with his children, told the lansquenets in the doorway as he went by that they needn't bother to come along, lifted the boys into the wagon, and kissed and comforted his tearful little girls whom he had ordered to stay behind with the old servant's daughter. No sooner had he himself climbed into the wagon than the official with his following of constables came out of the house across the way and asked him where he was going. On Kohlhaas' answering that he was going to Lockewitz to see his friend the steward, who a few days ago had invited him and his two boys to visit him in the country, the official said that in that case he must ask Kohlhaas to wait a minute or so, as he would be accompanied by some mounted lansquenets in obedience to the Prince of Meissen's orders. Kohlhaas looked down with a smile from the wagon and asked

him if he thought his life would not be safe in the
house of a friend who had invited him to share his
board for the day. The official replied good-humoredly that the danger was certainly not very great, adding
that the soldiers were not to incommode him in any
way. Kohlhaas, now looking grave, answered that on
his coming to Dresden the Prince of Meissen had left
it up to him as to whether he should have the guard or
not; when the official expressed surprise at this, and
in carefully chosen words reminded him that he
had been accompanied by the guard all the time he
had been there, the horse dealer described the circumstances under which the soldiers had been put
into his house. The official assured him that by order
of the Governor of the Palace, Baron von Wenk, who
was at the moment chief of police, he must keep an
uninterrupted watch over his person; if he would not
consent to the escort, would he be good enough to go
to the Government House himself to clear up the misunderstanding that must certainly exist. Kohlhaas,
giving the man an expressive look, and his mind now
made up to settle the matter once and for all, said that
he would do just that; got down from his wagon with
beating heart; gave the children to the servant to take
back into the house; and, leaving the groom waiting in
front of the house with the carriage, went off to the
Government House with the official and his guard.

When the horse dealer entered with his escort,
he found the Governor of the Palace, Baron von
Wenk, in the middle of looking over a group of

Nagelschmidt's men who had been captured near Leipzig and brought to Dresden the evening before, while the knights with him questioned the fellows about a great many things that information was wanted on. The Baron, as soon as he caught sight of the horse dealer, went up to him in the silence that followed the sudden cessation of the interrogation and asked him what he wanted; and when the horse dealer respectfully explained his intention of going to dine at midday with the steward at Lockewitz, and said he wished to leave the lansquenets behind since he did not need them, the Baron changed color and, seeming to swallow something that he was about to say, told Kohlhaas that he would do well to stay quietly at home and postpone the spread at the Lockewitz steward's for the present. Then, turning to the official and cutting short the colloquy, he told him that the orders he had given him about Kohlhaas still held good and that the latter was not to leave the city unless accompanied by six mounted lansquenets. Kohlhaas asked him if he was a prisoner, and if he was to understand that the amnesty solemnly granted him before the eyes of the whole world was now broken, upon which the Baron wheeled around suddenly, thrust his face, which had flushed a fiery red, up to Kohlhaas', said, "Yes! Yes! Yes!"—turned his back on him again, left him standing where he was, and went back to the Nagelschmidt men. Whereupon Kohlhaas left the room. Although he realized that what he had done had made the only possibility now remaining to him—flight—much more difficult, nevertheless he did not regret it because he now felt released from any further obligation to observe the terms of the amnesty. Arriving home, he had the horses unharnessed and, feeling depressed and upset, went to his room, still accompanied by the official; and while the latter assured the horse dealer, in a way that sickened him, that all the trouble must be due to some misunderstanding which would shortly be cleared up, he signed to the constables to bolt all the doors leading to the courtyard; but the main entrance, he hastened to say, was still open for him to use as he pleased.

Meanwhile Nagelschmidt had been so hard pressed from every side by sheriff's men and lansquenets in the forests of the Erzgebirge that the idea occurred to him, seeing how he lacked all means to carry through the kind of role he had undertaken, of actually getting Kohlhaas to help him; and since a traveler passing that way had given him a fairly accurate notion of how matters stood with Kohlhaas' lawsuit in Dresden, he thought he could persuade the horse dealer, in spite of the open enmity between them, to seal a new alliance with him. He therefore sent one of his fellows to him with a letter, written in almost unreadable German, that said: If he would come to the Altenburg and resume command of the band they had got together there from the remnants of his dispersed troops, he, Nagelschmidt, was ready to help him escape from Dresden by furnishing him with horses, men, and money; at the same time he promised

Kohlhaas to be more obedient, indeed better behaved in every respect, in the future than he had been in the past; and to prove his faithfulness and attachment, he pledged himself to come in person to the outskirts of Dresden in order to rescue Kohlhaas from jail. Now the fellow whose job it was to deliver this letter had the bad luck, in a village right near Dresden, to fall down in a violent fit of a kind he was susceptible to from childhood; the letter that he was carrying in his tunic was discovered by the people who came to his aid, while he himself, as soon as he had recovered consciousness, was arrested and, followed by a large crowd, carried to the Government House under guard. As soon as Baron von Wenk had read the letter, he went to see the Elector at the Palace, and there he also found Sir Kunz (who was now recovered from his injuries), Sir Hinz, and the President of the Chancery of State, Count Kallheim. It was these gentlemen's opinion that Kohlhaas should be arrested without delay and tried for secretly conspiring with Nagelschmidt; for they pointed out that such a letter could not have been written unless there had been earlier letters from the horse dealer's side and unless a criminal compact had been concluded by the two for the purpose of hatching fresh iniquities. But the Elector steadfastly refused to violate, on the sole grounds of this letter, the safe-conduct he had solemnly promised Kohlhaas; he himself was inclined to think that Nagelschmidt's letter indicated there had been no previous connection between the two; and all he would consent to do to get to the bottom of the matter, though only after long hesitation, was, following the President's proposal, to let the letter be delivered to Kohlhaas by Nagelschmidt's man, just as if he had never been arrested, and see whether Kohlhaas would answer it. The next morning, accordingly, the fellow, who had been put in jail, was brought to the Government House where the Governor of the Palace gave him back the letter and ordered him to deliver it to the horse dealer as if nothing had happened, in return for which he promised him his freedom and to let him off the punishment he had earned. The fellow lent himself to this base deception forthwith, and in apparently mysterious fashion, on the pretext of selling crabs (which the official supplied him with from the market) he gained admission to Kohlhaas' room. Kohlhaas, who read the letter while the children played with the crabs, in other circumstances would certainly have seized the rascal by the collar and handed him over to the lansquenets at his door; but in the present temper of men's minds even such a step was liable to misconstruction, and anyhow he was fully convinced that nothing in the world could ever rescue him from the business in which he was entangled: So, looking mournfully into the fellow's face which he knew so well, he asked him where he was staying and told him to come back in an hour or so when he would let him know his decision. At his bidding Sternbald, who happened to come in the door of his room, bought some crabs from the man; when this was done, and both men had left without recognizing one another, Kohlhaas sat down and wrote Nagelschmidt as follows: First, that he accepted his offer to take command of the band in Altenburg; that Nagelschmidt should therefore send a wagon with two horses to Neustadt-near-Dresden so that he could make his escape with his five children; that, to get away faster, he would also need another team of two horses on the road to Wittenberg which, though a roundabout way, was the only one he could take to come to him, for reasons it would take too long to explain; that he thought he could bribe the lansquenets who were guarding him, but in case force was necessary he would like to be able to count on finding a pair of stout-hearted, capable, and well-armed fellows in Neustadt; that he was sending him twenty gold crowns by his messenger to pay the cost of all these preparations, and he would settle with him afterwards about the sums actually paid out; and that as for the rest, he requested Nagelschmidt not to come to Dresden to take a personal part in the rescue as it was unnecessary, indeed he explicitly ordered him to stay behind in Altenburg in temporary command of the band, which could not be left without a chief.

When the messenger returned in the evening Kohlhaas gave him the letter, accompanied by a generous tip, and warned him to guard it carefully.

Kohlhaas' intention was to go to Hamburg with his five children and there embark for the Levant or the East Indies or wherever the blue sky looked down on people entirely different from the ones he knew: For quite apart from his reluctance to make common cause with Nagelschmidt, in the despair and anguish of his soul he had given up hope of ever seeing his pair of blacks fattened by the Junker.

No sooner had the fellow delivered the horse dealer's answer to the Governor of the Palace than the Lord Chancellor was deposed, the President, Count Kallheim, was appointed head of the court in his place, and, by an order in council of the Elector, Kohlhaas was arrested, put in chains, and thrown into the Dresden dungeon. On the evidence of the letter, a copy of which was posted at every street corner, he was brought to trial; and when he answered "Yes!" to a councilor who held the letter up in front of him at the bar and asked him if he acknowledged the handwriting as his own, but looked down at the ground and said "No!" when he was asked if he had anything to say in his own defense, Kohlhaas was condemned to be tortured with red-hot pincers by knackers' men, to be drawn and quartered, and his body burned between the wheel and the gallows.

Thus matters stood with poor Kohlhaas in Dresden when the Elector of Brandenburg intervened to pluck him from the fist of arbitrary power; in a note presented to the Chancery of State in Dresden, he claimed him as a subject of Brandenburg. For the honest City Governor, Sir Heinrich von Geusau, during a walk on the banks of the Spree, had told the Elector the story of this strange person who was really not a bad man, and when closely questioned by the astonished sovereign about it he could not avoid indicating the heavy responsibility which his own royal person bore for the improper way in which his Archchancellor, Count Siegfried, had conducted himself. The Elector, extremely angry, called the Archchancellor to account, and, finding that his kinship with the house of Tronka was to blame for it all, he immediately relieved him of his post, with more than one token of his displeasure, and appointed Sir Heinrich von Geusau to his place.

Now just at this time the Polish crown was involved in a dispute with the House of Saxony, over what we do not know, and pressed the Elector of Brandenburg repeatedly to make common cause with them against the Saxons; and in this situation the Archchancellor, Sir Geusau, who did not lack for skill in such matters, saw an opportunity to satisfy his sovereign's desire to see justice done Kohlhaas without imperiling the peace of the whole realm more than consideration for one individual warranted. Accordingly, the Archchancellor not only insisted on Saxony's immediately and unconditionally surrendering Kohlhaas on account of the arbitrary proceedings used against him, which were an offense against God and man, so that the horse dealer, if he were guilty of a crime, could be tried according to the laws of Brandenburg on charges preferred by the Dresden court through an attorney in Berlin; but Sir Heinrich even demanded a passport for an attorney whom the

Elector of Brandenburg wished to send to Dresden to see that justice was done Kohlhaas in the matter of the black horses that the Junker Wenzel von Tronka took from him on Saxon territory, as well as other flagrant instances of ill-usage and acts of violence. The Chamberlain, Sir Kunz, who had been appointed President of the State Chancery in the change of posts in Saxony, and who in his present hard-pressed circumstances had a number of reasons for not wishing to offend the Berlin court, replying in the name of his sovereign, whom the note from Brandenburg had very much cast down, said: He wondered at the unfriendliness and the unfairness which Brandenburg showed in challenging the right of the Dresden court to judge Kohlhaas according to its laws for crimes he had committed on Saxon ground, since the whole world knew that the horse dealer owned a large piece of property in the capital and did not himself dispute the fact that he was a citizen of Saxony. But since the Polish crown was already assembling an army of five thousand men on the Saxon frontier to press their claims by arms, and since the Archchancellor, Sir Heinrich von Geusau, announced that Kohlhaasenbrück, the place after which the horse dealer was named, lay in Brandenburg and they would consider the execution of the death sentence on him as a violation of the law of nations, the Elector of Saxony, following the advice of the Chamberlain Sir Kunz himself (who wanted to withdraw from the whole business), summoned Prince Christiem of Meissen from his estates and decided, after a few words with this prudent man, to heed the Berlin court's demand and give Kohlhaas up. The Prince, little pleased with all the improprieties committed in the Kohlhaas affair but required by his hardpressed sovereign to take over its direction, asked the Elector on what grounds he now wished to act against the horse dealer in the High Court at Berlin; and since they could not base their case on Kohlhaas' unfortunate letter to Nagelschmidt because of the questionable and obscure circumstances under which it had been written, nor on all of Kohlhaas' earlier acts of depredation and arson for which he had been pardoned by edict, the Elector decided to furnish His Majesty the Emperor in Vienna with an account of Kohlhaas' armed invasion of Saxony, accuse him of breaking the Emperor's peace, and appeal to His Majesty, who was of course not bound by any amnesty, to have Kohlhaas arraigned by the Imperial prosecutor for these crimes before the High Court at Berlin. A week later the horse dealer, still in chains, was packed into a wagon by the Knight Friedrich von Malzahn, whom the Elector of Brandenburg had sent to Dresden with six horsemen, and, reunited with his five children who had been collected at his plea from various foundling homes and orphan asylums, he was carried toward Berlin.

Now just at this time the Elector of Saxony, at the invitation of the High Bailiff, Count Aloysius von Kallheim, who in those days owned broad estates along the Saxon border, had gone to a great stag hunt at Dahme that had been got up for his entertainment, and in his company were the Chamberlain Sir Kunz and his wife Lady Heloise, daughter to the High Bailiff and sister to the President, not to mention other brilliant lords and ladies, hunting pages, and courtiers. Under the shelter of tents streaming pennants that were pitched right across the road on a hill, the entire company, still covered with the dust of the hunt, were seated at table and being served by pages, while lively music sounded from the trunk of an oak tree, when Kohlhaas and his escort of horsemen came riding slowly up the road from Dresden. For the illness of one of his little children, who were quite frail, had made it necessary for the Knight of Malzahn to hold up for three days in Herzberg; a measure which, as he was answerable only to the Prince he served, the Knight had seen no need to inform the Dresden government about. The Elector, with his shirt open at the throat and his feathered hat stuck with sprigs of fir in hunter's fashion, was seated beside the Lady Heloise, who had been the first love of his youth, and the gaiety of the fête having put him in a high good humor, he said, "Let's go and offer this goblet of wine to the unfortunate fellow, whoever he may be." Lady Heloise, giving him a splendid look, immediately got up and levied tribute on the whole table to fill a silver dish handed her by a page with fruit, cakes, and bread; and the entire company had already streamed out of the tent with refreshments of every kind in their hands when the High Bailiff came toward them in evident embarrassment and begged them to stay where they were. When the Elector asked him in

102

HEINRICH VON KLEIST

surprise what had happened to throw him into such confusion, the Bailiff, looking at the Chamberlain, stammered out that it was Kohlhaas who was in the wagon; at this piece of news, which none could understand, for it was public knowledge that the horse dealer had departed six days ago, the Chamberlain, Sir Kunz, turning back toward the tent, emptied his goblet of wine into the sand. The Elector, flushing violently, set his goblet down on a plate that a page held out to him at a sign from the Chamberlain; and while the Knight Friedrich von Malzahn, respectfully saluting the company whom he did not know, passed slowly through the tent ropes running across the road and continued on his way toward Dahme, the ladies and gentlemen, at the Bailiff's invitation, returned inside the tent. The Bailiff, as soon as the Elector was seated again, secretly sent a messenger to Dahme to tell its magistrate to see to it that the horse dealer was speeded on his way; but as the day was too far gone and the Knight of Malzahn insisted on spending the night there, there was nothing for it but to put Kohlhaas up, very quietly, at one of the magistrate's farmhouses, which lay hidden in the thickets off the main road. Toward evening, when all recollection of the incident had been driven from the lords' and ladies' minds by the wine and sumptuous desserts, the High Bailiff announced that a herd of stags had been sighted and proposed that they should take their stations again, a proposal that the whole company eagerly took up. Getting guns for themselves, they

hurried, in pairs, over ditches and hedges, into the
nearby forest—which was how it happened that the
Elector and the Lady Heloise, who had taken his arm
to go and watch the sport, found to their astonishment
that their guide had led them right into the yard of the
house in which Kohlhaas and the Brandenburg horsemen were lodged. Lady Heloise, when she heard this,
said, "Come, your Highness," playfully tucking the
chain that hung around the Elector's neck inside his
silk tunic, "let's slip inside the farmhouse before the
crowd catches up and see what the strange man spending the night there is like!" The Elector, reddening,
caught hold of her hand and said, "Heloise, what are
you saying?" But when she looked at him in surprise
and said there was no fear of his being recognized in
the hunting clothes he was wearing, and pulled him
along, and when at that very moment a pair of hunting
pages who had already satisfied their curiosity came
out of the house and reported that neither the Knight
nor the horse dealer, thanks to the High Bailiff's
efforts, knew who the company gathered in the neighborhood of Dahme were, the Elector pulled his hat
down over his eyes with a smile and said, "Folly rules
the world, and her throne is a pretty woman's lips!"

The nobleman and lady entered to find Kohlhaas
sitting on a heap of straw with his back against the
wall, in the midst of feeding bread and milk to the
child who had fallen ill at Herzberg. Lady Heloise,
to start a conversation, asked him who he was and
what was the matter with the child, and what he had

done, and where were they taking him with such an escort, to all of which Kohlhaas, doffing his leather cap, gave short but sufficient answers as he went on feeding his child. The Elector, who was standing behind the hunters, noticed a little lead capsule hanging from a silk string around the horse dealer's neck, and for lack of anything better to say he asked him what it meant to him and what was in it. "This capsule, your Worship!" Kohlhaas replied, and he slipped it from around his neck, opened it, and drew out a little piece of paper sealed with gum—"There is a very strange story connected with this capsule. Seven months ago, I think it was, the very next day after my wife's funeral—I had left Kohlhaasenbrück, as you perhaps know, to capture the Junker von Tronka, who had done me a very grave injustice—the Elector of Saxony and the Elector of Brandenburg met to discuss some business, though exactly what it was I do not know, in the market town of Jüterbock, through which my expedition led me; and having satisfactorily settled matters between them by evening, they walked along in friendly conversation through the streets of the town to see the merrymaking at the fair, which happened to be taking place just then. In the market square they came upon a gypsy woman sitting on a stool, telling the fortunes of the people standing around her, and they asked her jokingly if she didn't also have something to tell them that they would like to hear. I had just dismounted with my men at an inn and was present in the square when all this happened, but as I was standing at the rear of the crowd, in the entrance to a church, I could not make out what the strange woman said to the two lords; and when the people, whispering laughingly to their neighbors that she did not share her knowledge with everybody, crowded in close to witness the scene about to take place, I got up on a bench behind me that was hewn out of the church entrance, really not so much because I was curious myself as to make room for the curious. No sooner did I catch an interrupted view, from this vantage point, of the two lords and the old woman, who was sitting on the stool in front of them and seemed to be scribbling something, than she stood up suddenly on her crutches and, searching around the crowd, fixed her eye on me, who had never exchanged a word with her nor ever in all my life desired to consult her art; making her way through the dense throng, she said, 'There! If the gentleman wishes to know his fortune he may ask you about it!' And with these words, Your Worship, she handed me this paper in her shriveled, bony hands. And when I said in astonishment, as all the people turned to look at me, 'Granny, what's this present you are giving me?' she answered, after mumbling a lot of stuff I couldn't make out, in the middle of which, however, I was flabbergasted to hear her say my own name, 'An amulet, Kohlhaas the horse dealer; take good care of it, some day it will save you your life!'—and she vanished. Well," Kohlhaas continued good-naturedly, "to tell the truth, I had a pretty close call in Dresden,

106

HEINRICH VON KLEIST

but still I got off with my skin. But how I shall make out in Berlin, and whether the charm will come to my rescue there too, the future must show."

At these words the Elector dropped down on a bench; when Lady Heloise asked him anxiously what was the matter with him, he answered, "Nothing, nothing at all," only to collapse unconscious on the floor before she could spring forward and catch him in her arms. The Knight of Malzahn entered the room just then on an errand and said, "Good God, what's wrong with the gentleman?" Lady Heloise cried, "Fetch some water!" The pages lifted the Elector up and laid him on a bed in the next room; and the consternation reached its height when the Chamberlain, who had been summoned by a page, declared, after several vain attempts to restore him to consciousness, that he gave every sign of having suffered a stroke. The Bailiff, while the Cupbearer sent a courier on horseback to Luckau for the doctor, had the Elector, after he had opened his eyes, put in a carriage and carried at a walk to his hunting lodge nearby; but the ride was responsible for his falling into two more fainting fits after he had arrived there, and it was not until late the next morning, after the doctor from Luckau had arrived, that he recovered somewhat, though showing definite symptoms of the onset of a nervous fever. As soon as he was fully conscious again, the Elector raised himself on his elbow and his first question was: Where was Kohlhaas? The Chamberlain, misunderstanding the question, took his hand and said he could set his mind at rest about that dreadful man: After that strange and inexplicable occurrence, he himself had given orders for Kohlhaas to remain where he was in the farmhouse at Dahme with his escort from Brandenburg. Assuring the Elector of his wannest sympathy, and protesting how bitterly he had taxed his wife for her irresponsible frivolity in bringing him together with that man, the Chamberlain asked his master what had produced such a strange and awful effect on him in the interview. He had to confess, the Elector replied, that it was the sight of an insignificant piece of paper the man carried about with him inside a lead capsule that was to blame for the whole unpleasant incident. He added a great deal more besides by way of explanation, which the Chamberlain could not understand; suddenly swore to him, as he clasped his hand in his own, that his possessing the paper was of the utmost consequence to him; and begged him to mount that instant, ride to Dahme, and get it for him from the horse dealer at whatever cost. The Chamberlain, who had difficulty in concealing his dismay, assured him that if the piece of paper had the slightest value to him, nothing in the world was more essential than to hide that fact from Kohlhaas: If an indiscreet remark made the latter suspect something, all the Elector's riches would not suffice to buy it from that ferocious fellow with his insatiable vindictiveness. To reassure the Elector, he added that they must think of another way, and since the scoundrel probably did not set much store by the paper for its own sake, perhaps they could trick him into giving it up to some third person who had never had any part in the matter. The Elector, wiping his sweating face, asked if they might not send somebody to Dahme right away to try and do that, and meanwhile they could keep the horse dealer from going on until the paper was got hold of somehow. The Chamberlain, who could hardly believe his ears, answered that unfortunately, by every reckoning, the horse dealer must already have left Dahme and got across the border onto Brandenburg ground, where any attempt to interfere with his going on or to make him turn back would create exceedingly unpleasant and in all likelihood insurmountable difficulties. As the Elector fell back mutely on the pillow with a look of utter despair, the Chamberlain asked him what was in the paper and by what strange and inexplicable chance he had found out that the contents concerned himself. To this, however, the Elector gave no answer, only looking suspiciously at the Chamberlain, whose obligingness he was beginning to distrust; he lay there rigid, his heart beating nervously, staring down abstractedly at the corner of the handkerchief he was holding in his hands, when suddenly he asked the Chamberlain to summon the Junker von Stein, an energetic, clever young man whom he had often employed before in affairs of a secret nature, on the pretext that he had some other business to arrange with him. After explaining the matter to von Stein and impressing upon him the importance of the paper in Kohlhaas' possession, the Elector asked him if he wished to acquire an eternal claim on his friendship by getting hold of the paper for him before the horse dealer reached Berlin; and when the Junker, as soon as he had somewhat grasped the situation, which in truth was a very strange one, promised to serve him to the utmost of his ability, the Elector commanded him to ride after Kohlhaas and, since there was little likelihood of his being got at with money, to make him a shrewd speech and offer him his life and liberty in exchange for the paper—indeed, if Kohlhaas insisted on it, he should help him then and there, with horses, men and money, albeit prudently, to escape from the Brandenburg horsemen. The Junker, after requesting a letter of credentials which the Elector wrote out for him, immediately set out with several men, and, as he did not spare the horses, he was lucky enough to overtake Kohlhaas in a border village where the horse dealer, his five children, and the Knight von Malzahn were eating their midday meal in the open air before the door of a house. The Knight of Malzahn, on the Junker's introducing himself as a passing stranger who wished to catch a glimpse of his extraordinary prisoner, at once made him acquainted with Kohlhaas and courteously invited him to be seated; and since the Knight was coming and going continually in his preparations to leave, and the troopers were eating their dinner on the other side of the house, the Junker soon found an opportunity to tell the horse dealer who he was and the special business he came to him on.

The horse dealer already knew the title and name of the man who had swooned in the farmhouse at Dahme at the sight of the lead capsule and all he needed to climax the excitement into which this discovery had thrown him was to open the paper and read its secrets; but this, for various reasons, he was determined not to do for mere curiosity's sake. Replying to the Junker, he said that, in view of the ungenerous and unprincely treatment he had been forced to endure in Dresden despite his entire willingness to make every possible sacrifice, he would keep the paper. When the gentleman asked him why he gave this strange refusal to a proposal involving nothing less than his life and liberty, Kohlhaas said, "Noble sir, if your sovereign should come to me and say, 'I'll destroy myself and the whole pack of those who help me wield the scepter'—destroy himself, mind you, which is the dearest wish of my soul—I would still refuse him the paper, which is worth more to him than his life, and say, 'You can send me to the scaffold, but I can make you suffer, and I mean to.'" And Kohlhaas, with death staring him in the face, called a trooper over and invited him to have the large portion of food left in his dish. And all the rest of the hour that he spent in the place he behaved as if the Junker sitting at the table were not there, only turning to give him a parting glance when he climbed into the wagon.

The Elector's condition took such a turn for the worse on his receiving this news that for three critical days the doctor feared for his life. But thanks to the fundamental soundness of his constitution he recovered at the end of several painful weeks on a sickbed; or at least he was well enough to be placed in a carriage amply supplied with pillows and robes and carried back to Dresden to take up the affairs of government again. No sooner did he arrive in the city than he summoned Prince Christiem of Meissen and inquired how far along the arrangements were for the departure for Vienna of the attorney Eibenmayer, whom the government intended sending there as its legal representative to accuse Kohlhaas before his Imperial Majesty of breach of the peace of the Empire. The Prince replied that, pursuant to the Elector's orders on his departing for Dahme, the attorney had left for Vienna immediately after the arrival in Dresden of the jurist Zäuner, whom the Elector of Brandenburg had commissioned to proceed against the Junker Wenzel von Tronka in the matter of Kohlhaas' black horses.

The Elector, walking over to his desk with a flushed face, expressed surprise at such haste, for he thought he had made it clear that he wanted Eibenmayer's departure postponed until after a consultation they needed to have with Dr. Luther, who had procured the amnesty for Kohlhaas, when he meant to issue a more definitive order. As he said this, he shuffled together some letters and documents lying on his desk with an expression of suppressed annoyance. The Prince, after a pause in which he looked at him in surprise, said that he was sorry if he had displeased him in this matter; however, he could show him the Council of State's decision requiring him to send the attorney off at the aforesaid time. He added that nothing had been said in the Council about a consultation with Dr. Luther; earlier in the affair it might perhaps have served some purpose to give consideration to the churchman's views because of his intercession on Kohlhaas' behalf, but this was no longer the case now that the amnesty had been broken before the eyes of the whole world and the horse dealer had been arrested and handed over to the Brandenburg courts for sentencing and execution. Well, the Elector remarked, the mistake of sending Eibenmayer off was really not too serious; however, for the present, until further orders from himself, he did not wish the man to bring the action against Kohlhaas in Vienna, and he requested the Prince to send a courier to him immediately with instructions to that effect. Unfortunately, the Prince replied, this order came a day too late, as Eibenmayer, according to a report he had just received, had already gone ahead and presented his complaint to the State Chancery in Vienna. "How was all this possible in so short a time?" the Elector asked in dismay, to which the Prince replied that three weeks had already passed since Eibenmayer's departure and his instructions had been to settle the business with all possible dispatch as soon as he arrived in Vienna. Any delay, the Prince added, would have been all the more unseemly, seeing how the Brandenburg attorney, Zäuner, was pressing his case against the Junker Wenzel von Tronka with stubborn persistence; he had already made a motion for the court to remove the horses from the hands of the knacker for the time being, with a view to their being ultimately restored to health, and, in spite of all his opponent's objections, he had won his point. The Elector rang the bell, saying never mind, it did not matter, and after turning back to the Prince and asking him, with a show of unconcern, how things were going in Dresden otherwise, and what had happened in his absence, he lifted his hand and, unable to conceal his inner distress, signalled him to go. That same day the Elector sent the Prince a note asking for the entire Kohlhaas file, on the pretext that the political importance of the case required him to give it his personal attention; and since he could not bear to think of destroying the one man who could tell him the paper's secrets, he wrote a letter in his own hand to the Emperor beseeching him with all his heart, for weighty reasons that he would perhaps be able to explain at greater length a little later on, to be allowed to withdraw for a time the accusation made against Kohlhaas by Eibenmayer. The Emperor, in a note drawn up by the State Chancery, replied as follows: He was astonished at the Elector's apparently sudden change of mind; the report that Saxony had furnished him on the Kohlhaas case made it a matter for the entire Holy Roman Empire; he consequently felt it his duty as Emperor to appear as Kohlhaas' accuser before the House of Brandenburg; and since the Court Justiciary, Franz Müller, had already gone to Berlin as the Emperor's advocate for the purpose of accusing Kohlhaas of breach of the public peace, retreat was no longer possible and the affair must take its course according to the law.

The Emperor's letter disheartened the Elector completely. When word reached him privately from Berlin a short time after that the action had been commenced before the High Court, and that Kohlhaas would in all probability end on the scaffold, the unhappy prince, resolving on one more effort, wrote a letter in his own hand to the Elector of Brandenburg in which he begged him to spare the horse dealer's life. He gave the pretext that the amnesty granted the man did not, in justice, permit a death sentence to be executed on him; assured the Elector that, in spite of the apparent severity with which Kohlhaas had been treated in Saxony, it had never been his intention to let him die; and described how inconsolable he would feel if the protection Berlin had said it wished to extend to the man should, by an unexpected turn of events, prove worse for him in the end than if he had remained in Dresden and his case had been decided according to Saxon law. The Elector of Brandenburg, to whom much in this account seemed ambiguous and obscure, answered that the vigor with which His Majesty's counsel was proceeding made any departure from the strict letter of the law in order to satisfy his wish absolutely out of the question. The misgivings that he had expressed about the justice of the proceeding were really excessive: For though the Elector of Saxony had granted Kohlhaas an amnesty for the offenses of which he now stood accused before the High Court in Berlin, it was not he who was the accuser but the Supreme Head of the Empire, whom the amnesty in no way bound. At the same time he pointed out how necessary it was, in view of Nagelschmidt's continuing outrages, which the outlaw, with unheard of audacity, had even carried as far as Brandenburg, to make an example of Kohlhaas; and asked him, in case he was not swayed by these considerations, to appeal to the Emperor himself, since an edict of reprieve for Kohlhaas could only be proclaimed by His Majesty.

The Elector fell ill again from chagrin and vexation over all these unsuccessful efforts; and when the Chamberlain visited his bedside one morning, he was moved to show him the letters he had written to Vienna and Berlin in his efforts to obtain a reprieve for Kohlhaas and in that way gain some time in which to try to get hold of the paper in the latter's possession. The Chamberlain fell on his knees in front of him and pleaded in the name of everything he held sacred and precious to tell him what the paper said. The Elector asked him to bolt the door and sit on his bed; and after taking his hand and pressing it to his heart with a sigh, he began as follows: "Your wife, I gather, has already told you how the Elector of Brandenburg and I encountered a gypsy woman on the third day of our meeting in Jüterbock. Now the Elector, who has a very lively spirit, had decided to play a joke on the bizarre old woman and ruin her reputation for soothsaying, which had just been all the talk at dinner, in front of all the people. Walking up to her table with folded arms, he demanded a sign from her, one that could be put to the proof that very day, to confirm the truth of the fortune she should tell him; otherwise, he declared, though she were the Roman Sibyl herself, he would not believe one word she said. The woman, measuring us at a glance from head to foot, said that this was the sign: The big horned roebuck that the gardener's son was raising in the park would come to meet us in the market place where we were standing, before we should have gone away. Now the roebuck, you must understand, was intended for the Dresden kitchen and was kept under lock and key inside an enclosure surrounded by high palings and shaded by the oaks of the park; and since the park as a whole, as well as the garden leading into it, was also kept carefully locked because of the smaller game and the fowl they contained, it was impossible to see how the beast could fulfill the strange prediction and come to meet us in the square. Nevertheless, the Elector was afraid there was some trick in it, and after a short consultation with me, since he was absolutely bent on exposing the ridiculousness of everything she had to say, he sent to the castle and ordered the roebuck slaughtered then and there and the carcass dressed for dinner on one of the next days. Then, turning back to the woman, before whom all this had been openly done, he said, 'Well, now! What kind of fortune have you got to tell me?' The woman studied his palm and said, 'Hail, my Elector and Sovereign! Your Grace shall rule for many years, the house from which you spring shall endure for many years, and your descendants shall be great and glorious and more powerful than all the other princes and sovereigns of the earth!'

"For a brief moment the Elector looked thoughtfully at the woman, then muttered in an undertone, as he took a step toward me, that now he almost regretted sending a messenger to stop the prophecy from coming true; and while the knights who followed him, amid loud rejoicing, showered money into the woman's lap, to which he added a gold piece from his own pocket, he asked her whether the greeting that she had for me had as silvery a sound as his. The woman, after opening a box at her side, very deliberately arranging the money in it according to kind and quantity, and then closing it again, shaded her eyes with her hand as if the sun annoyed her and looked at me; and when I repeated the question to her, and jokingly added to the Elector, while she studied my hand, 'She has nothing very pleasant to say to me, it seems,' she seized her crutches, laboriously raised herself up from the stool by them, and, pressing close to me with her hands held out mysteriously in front of her, she whispered distinctly in my ear, 'No!'

" 'Is that so?' I said in confusion, recoiling a step before her cold and lifeless look, which seemed to come from eyes of marble, as she sat down again on the stool behind her. 'From what direction does the danger to my house come?' Taking charcoal and paper and crossing her knees, she asked whether she should write it down for me; and when I said, 'Yes, please do,' because I was really at a loss and there was simply nothing else for me to say under the circumstances, she replied, 'All right. I will write down three things for you: the name of the last ruler your house shall have, the year in which he shall lose his throne, and the name of the man who shall seize it for himself by force of arms.' And having done so under the eyes of the crowd, she arose, sealed the paper with gum that she moistened in her wrinkled mouth, and pressed it with a leaden signet ring that she wore on her middle finger. And when I reached for the paper, more curious than words can express, as you may well imagine, she said, 'No, no, no, your Highness!' turned, and pointed with one of her crutches. 'From that man there, the one with the feathered bonnet, standing on the bench in the church entrance, behind all the people—get the paper back from him, if you like!' And before I could quite understand what she was saying, she turned around and left me standing speechless with astonishment in the square; clapping shut the box behind her and slinging it over her shoulder, she vanished into the crowd, and that was the last I saw of her. But at that very moment, I confess to my immense relief, the knight whom the Elector had sent to the castle reappeared and reported to him, with a broad grin, that two hunters had killed the roebuck under his very eyes and hauled it off to the kitchen. The Elector jovially put his arm through mine with the intention of leading me from the square, and said, 'Well, do you see? Her prophecy was just an ordinary swindle, not worth the time and money it cost us!' But what was our surprise when a shout went up, even before these words were fairly out of his mouth, all around the square, and everybody turned to see a huge butcher's dog trotting toward us from the castle yard with the roebuck that he had seized by the neck in the kitchen as fair game; and, hotly pursued by the kitchen menials, he let it fall to the ground three paces from us—and so in fact the woman's prophecy, which had been her pledge for the truth of everything she said, was fulfilled, and the roebuck, dead though it was, to be sure, had come to meet us in the market place.

"The lightning that plummets from a winter's sky is no more devastating than this sight was to me, and my first endeavor, as soon as I got free of the people around me, was to discover the whereabouts of the man with the feathered bonnet whom the woman had pointed out to me; but none of my people, though they searched without stop for three days, could discover even the remotest trace of his existence. And then, friend Kunz, a few days ago, in the farmhouse at Dahme, I saw the man with my own eyes!" And letting go the Chamberlain's hand and wiping his sweating face, he fell back on the couch.

The Chamberlain, who thought it a waste of effort to try and convince the Elector of his own very different view of this incident, urged him to use any and every means to get hold of the paper, and afterwards to leave the fellow to his fate; but the Elector said that he saw absolutely no way of doing so, although the thought of having to do without the paper, or perhaps see all knowledge of it perish with the man, nearly drove him out of his mind. When his friend asked him if he had made any attempt to find the gypsy woman, the Elector said that he had ordered the Government to search for her, on some pretext or other, throughout the length and breadth of the Electorate, which they had been doing to this very day without result, but that for reasons he would rather not go into he doubted whether she could ever be found in Saxony. Now it happened that the Chamberlain intended to visit Berlin to see about a number of large properties in Neumark that his wife had inherited from Count Kallheim, whose death had followed upon his dismissal from the Chancellorship; and as he really loved the Elector, he asked him, after a moment's reflection, if he would allow him a free hand with the whole business. When his master pressed his hand warmly to his breast and said, "Be myself in this, and get me the paper!" the Chamberlain turned over his affairs of office, advanced his departure by several days and, leaving his wife behind, set out for Berlin accompanied only by a few servants.

Meanwhile Kohlhaas had arrived in Berlin, as we have said, and by special order of the Elector of Brandenburg was lodged in a knights' jail, where he and his five children were made as comfortable as circumstances permitted. As soon as the Imperial Attorney General from Vienna appeared, he was summoned to the bar of the High Court to answer the charge of breach of the peace of the Empire; and when he pleaded in his own defense that he could not be indicted for his armed invasion of Saxony and the acts of violence accompanying it because of the agreement he had made with the Elector of Saxony at Lützen, he was formally apprised that His Majesty the Emperor, whose Attorney General was the complainant in the case, could not give that any consideration. The matter having been explained to him in detail, however, and on his being assured that on the other hand full satisfaction would be given him in Dresden in his action against the Junker Wenzel von Tronka, he very soon yielded his defense. Thus it fell out that on the very day that the Chamberlain arrived in Berlin, sentence was pronounced and Kohlhaas was condemned to die on the block—a sentence which, in spite of its mercifulness, seeing how complicated the affair was, no one believed would be carried out, which indeed the whole city, knowing the goodwill the Elector bore Kohlhaas, confidently expected to see commuted to a simple, even if long and severe, term of imprisonment. The Chamberlain, who nevertheless understood that there was no time to be lost if he was to execute his master's commission, started out by showing himself to Kohlhaas in his ordinary court costume, clearly and close at hand, one morning when the horse dealer was standing at the window of his prison innocently studying the passers-by; and, concluding from a sudden movement of Kohlhaas' head that he had noticed him, and observing with particular satisfaction how his hand went involuntarily to the part of his chest where the capsule hung, he considered what had passed at that moment in Kohlhaas' soul as sufficient preparation for his going one step further in his attempt to get hold of the paper. He sent for an old woman that hobbled around on crutches selling old clothes, whom he had noticed in a crowd of other ragpickers in the streets of Berlin and who seemed to tally fairly well in her age and dress with the woman described to him by the Elector; and as he felt sure that the old gypsy woman's features had not impressed themselves very sharply on Kohlhaas' memory, since he had had only a fleeting glimpse of her as she handed him the paper, he decided to pass the one woman off as the other and have her masquerade, if possible, as the gypsy with Kohlhaas. To acquaint her with her part, he gave her a detailed account of everything that had taken place between the Elector and the gypsy woman, making sure, as he did not know how much the latter had revealed to Kohlhaas, to lay particular stress on the three mysterious items in the paper; and after explaining how she must mutter an incoherent and incomprehensible speech in which she would let it fall that schemes were afoot to get hold of the paper, on which the Saxon court set great importance, by force or cunning, he instructed her to pretend to Kohlhaas that the paper was no longer safe with him and to ask him to give it into her keeping for a few critical days. The old-clothes woman consented at once to do what was asked of her, provided she received a large reward, a part of which she insisted on the Chamberlain's paying her in advance; and since some months ago she had made the acquaintance of the mother of Herse, the groom that fell at Mühlberg, and this woman had the Government's permission to visit Kohlhaas occasionally, it was an easy matter for her, a few days later, to slip something into the warder's palm and gain admission to the horse dealer.

Kohlhaas, indeed, on the woman's entering and his seeing the signet ring on her hand and a coral chain hanging around her neck, thought he recognized the same old gypsy woman who had handed him the paper in Jüterbock; but probability is not always on the side of truth, and something had happened here which we must perforce record but which those who may wish to question are perfectly free to do: The Chamberlain had committed a most colossal blunder, and in the old-clothes woman whom he had picked up in the streets of Berlin to impersonate the gypsy woman he had stumbled upon that very same mysterious gypsy woman whom he wished to have impersonated. At any rate, the woman told Kohlhaas, as she leaned on her crutches and patted the cheeks of the children, who, scared by her strange appearance, shrank back against their father, that she had returned to Brandenburg from Saxony some time ago, and hearing the Chamberlain incautiously ask in the streets of Berlin about the gypsy woman who had been in Jüterbock in the previous spring, she had immediately pressed forward and offered herself, under a false name, for the business that he wanted done. The horse dealer was so struck by the uncanny likeness he discovered between her and his dead wife that he was inclined to ask the old woman whether she was Lisbeth's grandmother; for not only did the features of her face, as well as her still well-shaped hands and the way she gestured with them as she spoke, remind him vividly of Lisbeth, but he even noticed a mole on her neck just like the one Lisbeth had had. Amid a confusion of thoughts such as he had seldom experienced, the horse dealer invited her to sit down and asked what business of the Chamberlain's she could possibly have with him. The Chamberlain, she said, as Kohlhaas' old dog sniffed around her knees and wagged his tail when she scratched his head, had instructed her to disclose to the horse dealer the three questions that were so important to the Saxon court, the mysterious answers to which were contained in the paper; to warn him of an envoy who was in Berlin for the purpose of obtaining it; and to ask him for the paper on the pretext that it was no longer safe in his bosom where he carried it. But, she said, the real reason for her coming was to tell him that the threat to get the paper away from him by force or cunning was an absurd and empty one; that he need not have the least fear for its safety while he was in the custody of the Elector of Brandenburg; that the paper, indeed, was much safer with him than with her; and that he should take care not to give it up to anybody, regardless of who it was or what the pretext. Nevertheless, she said in conclusion, he would be wise, in her opinion, to use the paper for the purpose she had given it to him at the Jüterbock fair: Let him lend a favorable ear to the offer that the Junker von

Stein had made him on the frontier and surrender the paper to the Elector of Saxony in return for his life and liberty. Kohlhaas, who exulted in the power given him to wound his enemy mortally in the heel at the very moment that it was treading him in the dust, replied, "Not for the world, Granny, not for the world!" squeezed the old woman's hand, and only wanted to know what the paper's answers were to the awful questions. The old woman lifted the youngest child, who had been squatting at her feet, onto her lap and said, "Not for the world, Kohlhaas the horse dealer, but for this pretty little fair-headed little boy!" and she smiled at the child and petted him as he looked at her wide-eyed, and with her bony hands gave him an apple from her pocket. Kohlhaas, disconcerted, said that the children themselves, when they were grown, would approve his conduct, and that he could do nothing better for them and for their grandchildren than to keep the paper. Besides, he asked, after what had happened to him, who was there to guarantee him against his being deceived a second time, and would he not in the end be fruitlessly sacrificing the paper to the Elector just as he had recently done his band of men at Lützen? "Once a man has broken his word to me, I never trust him again. Only a clear and unmistakable request from you can part me from this bit of writing, through which satisfaction has been given me so wonderfully for all that I have suffered." The old woman, putting the child down again, said that in many respects he was right and he could do just as he pleased. And she took hold of her crutches to leave. Kohlhaas again asked her what was in that marvelous paper; he was eager, he said—as she quickly interjected that of course he could open it, but it would be pure curiosity on his part—to find out about a thousand other things before she left: who she really was, how she had come by the knowledge she possessed, why she had refused to give the paper to the Elector, for whom it had been written, after all, and among so many thousands of people had handed it just to him, Kohlhaas, who had never wanted anything from her skill.

But just at that moment some police officers were heard mounting the stairs and the old woman, alarmed lest she be discovered in the place, said, "Goodbye, Kohlhaas, goodbye till we meet again, when there won't be one of these things you shall not know!" And turning toward the door, she cried, "Farewell, children, farewell!" kissed the little people one after the other, and vanished.

Meanwhile the Elector of Saxony, a prey to his despairing thoughts, had called in two astrologers, named Oldenholm and Olearius, who then enjoyed a considerable reputation in Saxony, to ask their advice about the mysterious piece of paper that was so important to him and his posterity; but when, after an earnest investigation lasting several days that they conducted in the Dresden palace tower, the men could not agree as to whether the prophecy aimed at the centuries to come or at the present time, with perhaps the Polish crown being meant, with whom relations were still very warlike, the uneasiness, not to say despair, in which this unhappy lord found himself, being only intensified by such learned disputes, finally reached a pitch that was more than his spirit could bear. And on top of it all, just at this time the Chamberlain sent word to his wife, who was about to follow him to Berlin, to break the news discreetly to the Elector before she left that after an unsuccessful attempt he had made with the help of an old woman who had not been heard of since, their hopes of ever getting hold of the paper in Kohlhaas' possession seemed very dim, seeing that the death sentence pronounced on the horse dealer had now at last been signed by the Elector of Brandenburg, after a complete review of the file of the case, and the day of execution fixed for the Monday after Palm Sunday—at which news the Elector shut himself up in his room like a lost soul, his heart consumed by grief, but on the third day, after sending a short note to the Government House that he was going to the Prince of Dessau's to hunt, suddenly disappeared from Dresden. Where he actually went, and whether in fact he arrived in Dessau, we shall not attempt to say, as the chronicles which we have compared oddly contradict and cancel one another on this point. This much, however, is certain: That at this very time the Prince of Dessau lay ill in Brunswick at his uncle Duke Heinrich's residence and was hardly in a state to go hunting, and that the next evening Lady Heloise arrived in Berlin to join her husband Sir Kunz the Chamberlain in the company of a certain Count von Königstein, whom she introduced as her cousin.

Meanwhile, at the Elector of Brandenburg's order, the death sentence was read to Kohlhaas, his chains were struck off, and the property deeds taken from him in Dresden were returned; and when the counselors assigned him by the court asked what disposition he wished to make of his possessions, he drew up a will, with the help of a notary, in favor of his children and appointed his honest friend the bailiff of Kohlhaasenbrück to be their guardian. Nothing could match the peace and contentment of his last days; for soon after, a special Electoral decree unlocked the dungeon in which he was kept to all his friends, of whom he had a great many in the city, who were free to visit him day and night. Indeed, he even had the satisfaction, one day, of seeing the theologian Jacob Freising enter his jail with a letter for him from Dr. Luther in the latter's own hand—without doubt a most remarkable missive, all trace of which, however, has been lost; and from the hands of his minister, in the presence of two Brandenburg deans who assisted him, he received the blessing of the Holy Communion.

And now the fateful Monday after Palm Sunday arrived, on which Kohlhaas was to make atonement to the world for his all-too-rash attempt to take its justice into his own hands, amid a general commotion in the city which could not disabuse itself even yet of the hope of seeing him saved by an Electoral pardon. Just as he was passing out of the gate of the jail under a strong escort, with the theologian Jacob Freising leading the way and his two little boys in his arms (for he had expressly asked this favor at the bar of the court), the castellan of the Electoral palace came up to Kohlhaas through the crowd of grieving friends around him who were shaking his hand and saying goodbye, and with a haggard face handed him a paper that he said an old woman had given him. Kohlhaas stared in surprise at the man, whom he hardly knew, and opened the paper; its gum seal bore an impression that instantly recalled the gypsy woman. But who can describe the astonishment that gripped him when he read the following communication: "Kohlhaas, the Elector of Saxony is in Berlin; he has already gone ahead of you to the place of execution and can be recognized, if that is of any interest to you, by the hat with blue and white plumes he has on. I don't have to tell you what his purpose is: As soon as you are buried he is going to dig the capsule up and read the paper inside it. Your Elizabeth."

Kohlhaas, completely dumbfounded, turned to the castellan and asked him if he knew the mysterious woman who had given him the note. But just as the castellan answered: "Kohlhaas, the woman——" and then halted strangely in the middle of his sentence, the procession, starting up again, swept the horse dealer along and he was unable to make out what the man, who seemed to be trembling in every limb, was saying.

When he arrived at the scaffold, he found the Elector of Brandenburg and his suite, which included the Archchancellor Sir Heinrich von Geusau, sitting their horses in the midst of an immense crowd of people; on the Elector's right stood the Imperial Attorney General, Franz Müller, with a copy of the death sentence in his hand; on his left, his own attorney, Anton Zäuner, with the Dresden court's decree; in the center of the half-open circle, which the crowd completed, stood a herald with a bundle of articles in his hand, and the two black horses, sleek with health and pawing the ground with their hooves. For the action that the Archchancellor Sir Heinrich had started at Dresden in his master's name against the Junker Wenzel von Tronka having triumphed in every point, without the slightest reservation, a banner had been waved over the horses' heads to make them honorable again, they had been removed from the knacker's care, fattened by the Junker's men, and handed over, in the Dresden market place, to the horse dealer's attorney in the presence of a specially appointed commission. When Kohlhaas, with his guard, advanced up the knoll to the Elector, the latter said, "Well, Kohlhaas, this is the day on which justice is done you. Look here, I am giving you back everything that was taken from you by force at Tronka Castle, which I as your sovereign was duty bound to restore to you: the two blacks, the neckerchief, gold gulden, laundry—everything down to the money for the doctor's bills for your man Herse who fell at Mühlberg. Now are you satisfied with me?"

At a sign from the Chancellor the decree was handed to Kohlhaas, who set down the two children he was carrying on the ground and read it through with sparkling eyes; and when he found that it contained a clause condemning the Junker Wenzel von Tronka to two years' imprisonment, his feelings overcame him and, crossing his hands on his breast, he knelt down from afar before the Elector. Rising again and putting his hand in his bosom, he joyfully assured the Archchancellor that his dearest wish on earth had been fulfilled; walked over to the horses, examined them and patted their plump necks; and, coming back to the Chancellor, cheerfully announced that he was giving them to his two sons Heinrich and Leopold! The Archchancellor, Sir Heinrich von Geusau, looking down at him kindly from his horse, promised in the name of the Elector that his last wish would be held sacred, and also asked him if he would not dispose as he thought best of the things in the bundle. Kohlhaas thereupon called Herse's old mother, whom he had caught sight of in the square, out of the crowd, and, giving her the things, he said, "Here, Granny, these belong to you!"—adding the sum he had received as damages to the money in the bundle, as a gift to help provide for her in her old age.

The Elector called out, "Kohlhaas the horse dealer, now that satisfaction has been given you in this wise, you on your side prepare to satisfy His Majesty the Emperor, whose attorney stands right here, for breach of the public peace!" Taking off his hat and tossing it on the ground, Kohlhaas said he was ready to do so; he lifted the children from the ground one more time and hugged them tightly; then, giving them to the bailiff of Kohlhaasenbrück, who, weeping silently, led them away from the square with him, he advanced to the block. He had just unknotted his neckerchief and opened his tunic when he gave a quick glance around the circle formed by the crowd and caught sight, a short way off, of the figure that he knew with the blue and white plumes, standing between two knights whose bodies half hid him from view. Kohlhaas, striding up in front of the man with a suddenness that took his guard by surprise, drew out the capsule, removed the paper, unsealed it and read it through; and looking steadily at the man with the blue and white plumes, in whose breast fond hopes were already beginning to spring, he stuck the paper in his mouth and swallowed it. At this sight the man with the blue and white crest was seized by a fit and fell unconscious to the ground. Kohlhaas, however, while his dismayed companions bent over him and raised him from the ground, turned around to the scaffold where his head fell under the executioner's ax.

So ends the story of Kohlhaas. Amid the general lamentation of the people, his body was laid in a coffin; and while the bearers lifted it from the ground to carry it to the graveyard in the outskirts of the city for decent burial, the Elector of Brandenburg called the dead man's sons to him and, instructing the Archchancellor to enroll them in his school for pages, dubbed them knights on the spot. Shortly thereafter the Elector of Saxony returned to Dresden, shattered in body and soul; what happened subsequently there must be sought in history. Some hale and hearty descendants of Kohlhaas, however, were still living in Mecklenburg in the last century.